OF

GLASS

AND

CINDERS

KINGDOMS OF THE FAE

TIANI DAVIDS

To Grayson. This one doesn't have robots so it's fantasy.
Love you ;)

To the girls looking for strength, it's already in you.

Books by Tiani Davids

The Eldrasian Chronicles
The Dragon Healer
The Dragon Kin
The Dragon Queen

Kingdoms of the Fae
Of Swans and Princes (prequel novella)
Of Glass and Cinders

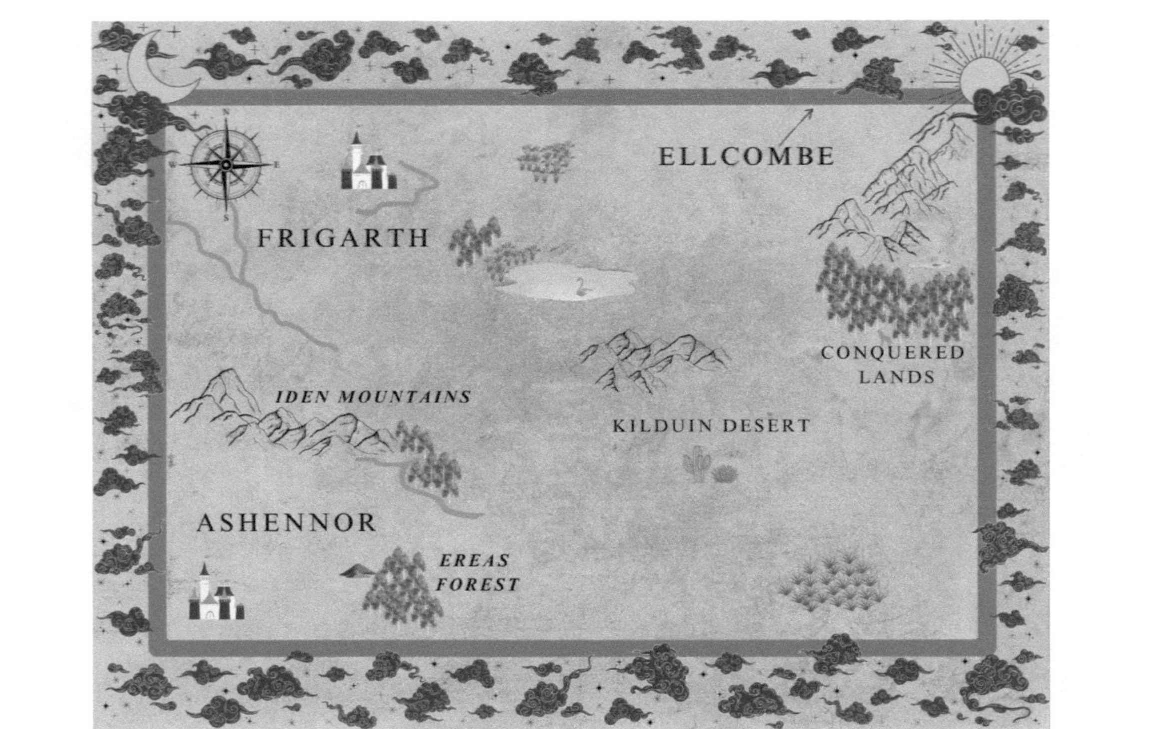

ELLCOMBE
FRIGARTH
CONQUERED LANDS
IDEN MOUNTAINS
KILDUIN DESERT
ASHENNOR
EREAS FOREST

1

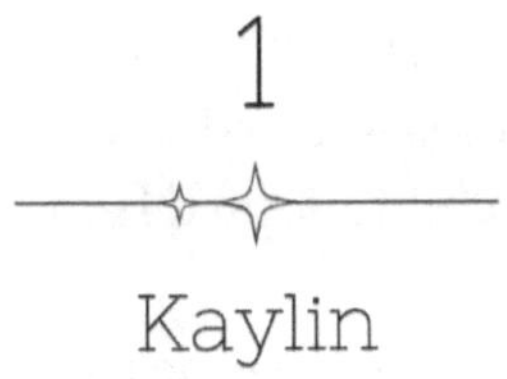

Kaylin

I'VE BEEN AWAKE AND dressed for nearly an hour, ready and waiting by the door, when I finally hear a rush of wind and the sound of the key turning in the lock.

My stomach still drops after all these years, memories flashing in my mind at the sound of Zianne's wind magic. Even though she can't do much more than mere flourishes without great strain, it's more than I could ever do.

I hurry from the room, not daring to make Zianne wait for me. The temperature difference hits me immediately. My room is the only fully enclosed part of the house. Made from large blocks of dark stone and barred by a thick wooden door—the only one in the whole building—the room is as cold as ice most mornings. It doubles as the root cellar, with crates of food taking up every inch around my bed and the small set of drawers housing my feeble collection of ragged clothes.

But Ashenor is a warm country, and the rest of the house is open to the sun and the already warm air. My shivers ease instantly as I pass through my doorway.

"Kaylin!" Zianne's voice barks from upstairs.

"Coming, Stepmother."

Stepmother. Zianne of course, is no such thing, but I learnt early on not to defy her. Especially when it helps her maintain the careful image she's crafted that I am not what I am. That I am not a slave, sold to her to cover my father's debts, but a human child adopted from the goodness of her fae heart.

I quietly scoff to myself. Zianne has no such goodness.

I shake my head as I hurry upstairs and into the open living room. Those thoughts do neither of us any good.

"Why aren't you in the kitchen preparing our breakfast?" Zianne says, her body draped delicately on the low couch, long hair flowing over her shoulder and revealing the delicate tips of her pointed ears.

I don't dare meet her cold grey eyes or point out that she only just unlocked my room. "I'm sorry, Stepmother. I'll get started now."

I can hear Oriane walking around her bedroom, and hurry into the kitchen. Oriane is the perfect mirror of her mother, right down to her grey eyes, high cheekbones, and cruel personality. I avoid them both as much as I can, but it's hard when there are no doors and so few walls.

But the kitchen offers a place of refuge as I bustle around preparing Zianne and Oriane's breakfast. Zianne had a screen built across the kitchen years ago when my father worked for her, hiding it from view of most of the house.

Humans should rarely be seen, and certainly never heard. At least while it suits her.

I emerge from the kitchen only ten minutes later, balancing three bowls in my hands.

"What took so long?" Oriane snaps, crossing the room to sit at the table. She looks exquisite, as usual. A light blue dress falls down to her knees, hugging her delicate frame and plunging low across her back. Her dark hair rests over her shoulder.

"I'm sorry," I say, placing the bowls on the oak table. It's a stunning piece, like everything Zianne owns—except me, of course. With intricate floral carvings across the top and winding down the legs. There are hints of starlight in it, as well.

Zianne seems to float across the room to sit opposite Oriane.

I pull a small jug of honey from the pocket of my apron and set it on the table before backing away.

They say nothing as they serve themselves generous helpings of the most expensive berries and fruits from across Ashennor and Frigarth Zianne could buy. My mouth waters.

But I don't move. I can't move until Zianne dismisses me. The seconds stretch on.

A gentle breeze blows through the room, a soft and warm caress on my skin. But Zianne shivers dramatically.

"Why haven't you started the fire yet, Kaylin? It's freezing in here."

Oriane's lips twitch in a barely concealed grin, a drop of juice staining the corner of her mouth.

"Sorry, Stepmother," I say, my eyes widening.

I hurry to the fireplace, piling the tinder and kindling high and striking the flint with expert ease. The fire instantly catches, and I coax it into a steady burn. My hand slips on a log, and a splinter sinks deep into my finger. Wincing, I shake my hand but keep piling the wood.

It has to be the only fire in all of Ashennor lit for the sole purpose of heating. Except perhaps deep inside the royal palace. But Zianne insists I light it daily.

Just another chore she's scraped up for me to complete. And the soot and dirt that covers me after a day of tending to it is just another thing she can criticise me for. I am too skinny, my blonde hair too lanky, my clothes too dirty, my movements dreadfully clumsy with humanness. She sees every fault.

As soon as the fire is going strong, I hurry back to the kitchen before Zianne can yell at me again. I haven't served her any iced tea yet.

Oriane's silky voice floats into the kitchen as I pour the fruity drink into two pitchers.

"Sarai simply couldn't stop talking about Jorai's birthday yesterday. She says the celebrations will last for *days*."

My back straightens and my hands still. Jorai. I strain my ears for any morsel of information about the prince.

Zianne is quiet, but I'm sure she's cocked her head thoughtfully. Her mind already racing with some kind of scheme.

"Rumour is," Oriane says conspiratorially, "he'll be looking for a *wife*."

I nearly drop the pitcher in my hand. Jory is already searching for a—a wife? I'm sure it's only his eighteenth they'll be celebrating.... I have to force my steps to slow as I go back into the room with their tea, hanging onto their every word.

"Then we'll have to be prepared, won't we? We can't have someone like Sarai claiming the prince's hand."

Oriane chuckles as I place a pitcher in front of her. She's four years older than Jorai, but such an age gap is nothing for the fae. Age is more of a ... concept for them. It's the appearance of the age that matters to most. Since the two appear close in age, they would be a fine match.

"Could you imagine that tramp with Jorai?"

"Hardly." Zianne waves her hand dismissively.

I open my mouth to ask for more about Jory but quickly bite my tongue. Zianne does not like to be reminded that my family—my *human* family— had ties to the palace. The fact that I knew Prince Jorai, heir to the Ashennor throne, as a child is a fact either steadfastly ignored or laughed at as the funniest of jokes. But the need to know more is almost overpowering.

"Mother," Oriane says, her voice turning sweet, "perhaps we should go shopping. You know, before the invitations go out and every girl in the city decides she needs a new dress."

Zianne's smile widens. "We'll have to look our best, after all. Kaylin!"

I jerk, my eyes snapping to Zianne.

"Clean this up. We're going to the markets. And get changed, I don't want that *thing* visible."

I glance down at the manacle steadfastly clamped around my left ankle, strips of cloth woven under it in a vain attempt to alleviate the rubbing. Once again, I bite down on my tongue, the urge to ask her to just remove it fighting its way up my throat.

But it's Zianne's favourite reminder of what awaits me if I disobey.

That, and the matching scars on my right ankle from where the other manacle used to be, linking my legs together with a too-short chain to stop me from running.

It didn't take long to work, especially when coupled with her other methods.

Instead, I nod and begin to gather up the dishes from the table as the two rise to prepare for their outing. The thought of finally, *finally* getting out of the house is enough to bring a smile to my face. It's been weeks since I was last allowed off the property.

But as Oriane reaches the light curtain shielding her room, I see her hand flick and a violent updraft of wind knocks the bowls from my hands. I try to catch them, but it's too late. They shatter on the stone floor.

A deadly quiet fills the room as the deafening crashes fade and Oriane slips into her bedroom. Zianne's silence settles over me like a thick, suffocating blanket. I don't dare raise my eyes to hers as I hurry to gather up the broken pieces.

"Stupid, clumsy girl! How dare you break my belongings!" Zianne screams, launching herself across the room. Her hand comes down hard across the side of my head, knocking me off balance and forcing me to catch myself with my hands. Glass instantly buries into my palms. "After all I have done for you! Taking you in when your father didn't want you. And *this* is what you do?"

I don't move. Waiting out the storm.

"Clean this up!" she snaps. "We're leaving as soon as Oriane is ready." And with one last slap across my head, she leaves the room.

Tears have blurred my eyes, and my ears are ringing, her words bouncing around my head, but I clean up the mess, carrying it into the kitchen and disposing of the fragments, before cleaning juice from the floor. My palms sting the entire time. But my comfort, as always, must wait.

It isn't until all trace of the mess I caused is gone that I can turn to my injured palms. Blood has pooled in the many lines of my hands, covering the calluses and even dripping down to my wrists. Biting my lip, I grab a pair of tweezers and set to work digging the glass from my skin. It only takes minutes, but tears have clouded my vision again by the time I'm finished.

I shouldn't care. I shouldn't be surprised. And she's right, my father didn't want me. But I wish ...

With a sigh, I drop my hands and hurry to my room. There's no time for wishes.

If I don't change into a dress long enough to hide the manacle, Zianne will be furious, and it could be another month before I'm allowed out.

2

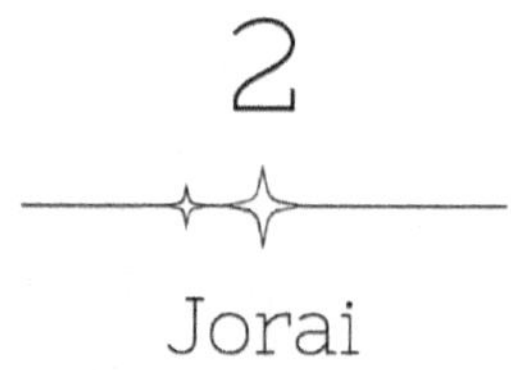

Jorai

I STRIDE DOWN THE starlight halls towards my father's sitting room with a deep sigh, the sun shining through the open arches and sprawling across the stone floor. Leaves crunch beneath my feet.

"I'm sure it's just a misunderstanding," I say, glancing at Zephi, Captain of the Royal Guard and my closest friend.

Zephi raises his dark eyebrows but says nothing, easily keeping pace with me.

"He knows how important this is."

"Yes, Your Highness."

I sigh again, a smile tugging at my lips. "Are you ever going to drop my title, Captain?"

"It wouldn't be proper, Your Highness," Zephi says, but his brown eyes glimmer with mirth.

I don't pause at the entrance to my father's sitting room, but I do nod to the guards stationed on either side of the starlight arch. Its glimmer is only faint during the day, but it still draws my eyes.

"Jorai!" my father's deep voice booms across the room. He sits behind his large oaken desk, piled high with an assortment of papers, parchments, and books.

A large opening behind him leads to a balcony that in turn lets out in a garden, featuring rows of heavily flowering plants coloured through the entire rainbow, stone benches, and a fae-made waterfall. Vines weave around the pillars, their leaves large and shaped like a teardrop.

Though my father is hundreds of years old, he still appears young, no more than the humans do at thirty. A benefit of our long life as fae.

"Father," I say, letting a note of my exasperation shine through as I stop opposite him. Zephi stands with the other guards.

The king frowns, sitting back in his chair.

"I've just been speaking with one of the organisers for the festival."

He raises an eyebrow. "And is everything suitable? These are your birthday celebrations!"

"Why does everyone seem to think it will be a fae-only event?" I say, crossing my arms.

Understanding flickers across my father's face.

"Jorai," he says, as though speaking to a young child, and though this is only my eighteenth birthday, the tone sends me bristling, "the humans won't *enjoy* a fae party. You know what they're like."

"We're all meant to be equal, Father. What was the point of the decree if we don't at least give them the option of coming? I'm sure there will be one or two who will attend."

Zephi shifts behind me but says nothing. I know what he'd say anyway. More than one or two will come. A lot more. These celebrations will be the biggest we've had in many years. Fae and humans will travel from all over Ashennor. Maybe even ...

I push the thought aside. I've not seen her in years, but I know she would love it all.

Nevertheless, my father says nothing.

I hesitate. "I've been hearing rumours, Father."

His eyes snap up to mine, a frown crinkling his brow. But then he dismisses whatever he heard in my tone and peers back down at his work. "There are no rumours, Jorai. It was a mere case of forgetfulness on my part. It'll take time to adjust. Things with the humans couldn't be better."

I know he's right. My father's decree to outlaw human slavery and raise them up to our level is still relatively new in our years. It's only been fifteen. It's only natural that they would still be forgotten occasionally. My father is a busy man.

The king's eyes, ice-blue like mine, turn thoughtful. "Of course they're invited. I'll send a reminder to the organising team. We don't want word travelling to our friends about this simple overlook."

I frown at the mention of Frigarth. "Thank you, Father."

"Now," he says, sitting back in his chair again, his full attention on me now. "There will be many influential young ladies there. I expect you to dance with all of them."

I repress a sigh. "Yes, Father."

"Any one of them would make a suitable match."

I feel my face heat but say nothing in response to this latest hint, and all thoughts of our neighbouring country fly from my mind.

My father is yet to officially announce my pursuit of a wife, or even *ask* me about it, but he has made more and more comments about the possibility recently. Regardless, none of the court women have caught my eye. None of them show any interest in me beyond the crown on my head. No one has in years. Their attentions might be flattering, but it's all in vain.

"Is that all, son?" Already, he's showing signs of distraction, his eyes trailing back to his paperwork. I've held him up too long.

I straighten. "That's all."

With a dismissive nod, he makes a mark on the paper in front of him, and I turn from the room.

Zephi is waiting for me, his face set in a guard's neutral expression. I hope he's feeling better too, now that he's heard my father's reassurances. Even if the prospect of a wife has sent my mind swirling.

Zephi falls into step beside me again as I set off back up the hall.

"I can't believe how forgetful he's been lately," I chuckle, trying to force thoughts of marriage from my mind, "but at least we got that straightened out."

Zephi is silent for a moment, long enough that I glance at him. His angular face is set in a frown.

"What?" I prod.

"I would hesitate to dismiss the rumours so quickly, Your Highness. I've heard many disturbing reports of abuse in the city. Even mention of slaves."

"I know the humans aren't my father's top priority right now, Zephi, but things *are* better for them. They're just rumours."

"Of course," Zephi says, but I can tell he's still not happy. "I'll meet up with you later, Your Highness. I'm late for my rounds."

"In the city?"

"Yes," he says, his eyes catching mine like he already knows what I'm going to ask.

"Keep an ear out for any gossip about the festival for me?" About my new search. Something tells me people will already know.

He gives a small bow of his head and turns away, stepping straight out into the sunshine. Most of the outer halls are open to the air, with pillars to support the roofing spaced occasionally throughout. Fae prefer to be outside as much as possible, even when we're *inside*.

I watch Zephi go, his hand resting on the hilt of his sword, and push his concerns from my mind. I'm not going to risk my father's displeasure over something I know he's already dealt with.

3

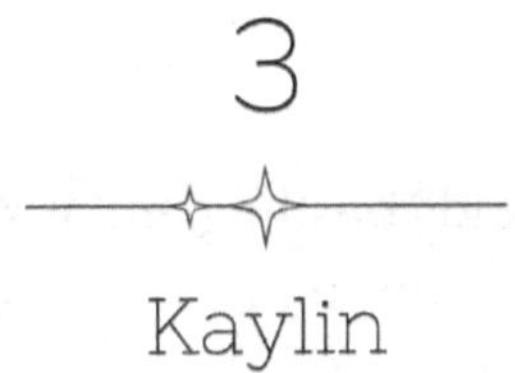

Kaylin

I N THAT MOMENT, STEPPING over the boundary line of Zianne's estate is like breathing air for the very first time. The sun is shining brightly overhead, and beads of sweat form on my forehead as I hurry after Zianne and Oriane, both riding equally beautiful white mares.

But my eyes are wide, drinking everything in. Ashennor hasn't changed much since I last saw it, but that just means it's as beautiful as before. The fae build their homes and buildings out of white and grey stone, but they're little more than pillars and roofs, with intricate carvings and flowers and vines decorating every inch of them. They love being in nature, and it shows.

Zianne's estate is a mere ten minutes from the city, with a stone road connecting straight to its heart. Homes grow closer together here. Some have curtains around their borders to offer privacy, others have vines netted together, while still others—like Zianne—don't care. I can see straight into their rooms, where some fae sit at tables and others are still lying in bed.

These fae will have removable screens for certain occasions when privacy demands it. I notice human dwellings dotted throughout. They've become harder to spot in recent years, as more and more embrace the fae custom of open homes now that conditions have improved for us. For them.

The market is already bustling, but it's not nearly as busy as it will be once the festival invitations go out. Oriane was right to suggest the trip today. Neat rows of stalls owned by both human and fae alike line the large court.

Many of the fae buyers are in their shifted forms: large cats, wolves, rabbits, deer, and so many others wander freely, while birds fly low over our heads and between bodies. But my eyes are pulled away from them and up to the palace.

It's a large, sprawling building, with only one level to keep as much of the interior as open as possible. Vines trail up the sides, with white and pink flowers decorating the reaching tendrils. During the day and under the rare cloud, it looks as though it is made from the same stone as the buildings surrounding us.

When the sun hits it, it glistens. But at night, their true nature is revealed. For the palace is made of starlight. A rare stone that shines a stunning, glittering silver beneath the moon.

It still feels like home. The palace. Though we never lived there, I spent much of my time inside with my mother—a maid—as she worked day in and day out. That's when I met Jory and his Aunt Cyra. Short for a fae, with curly blonde hair, she's as beautiful as she is kind.

There's little chance of seeing either of them today. There's no reason for them to come to the markets in person, a fact I'm sure Zianne is well aware of. I haven't seen either of them since—

"Kaylin!" Zianne snaps. She's twisted in the saddle, her beautiful face contorting with fury.

My eyes widen. She's waiting for me to help her dismount, and I've been staring at the palace like a fool. I grab the reins as she gracefully slides from the saddle.

When her feet hit the ground, she pulls me close as though for a hug, but her lips are by my ear. And only I can hear the words she says. They send a shiver down my spine, along my nerve endings, even through my very blood.

"You will not reveal who or what you are to anyone."

It's been weeks since Zianne used this specific magic, and I'm surprised she's dared to do so in public. Blood magic. This illegal power is the real reason that Zianne adopted me.

Because even magic has loopholes, and Zianne can always be trusted to find one.

Blood magic is widely believed to only work between relatives, because of their shared blood. Except magic is a tricky thing, and no one truly knows what it wants or means.

And so, blood magic works even when a piece of paper is all that deems the two related. Blood is still exchanged in the ritual, of course, and it is a weaker bond of power. Zianne's orders don't last nearly as long as they would if I had been her real daughter, and the strain upon her is greater, but it works nonetheless.

Anyone can complete the ritual, but few dare when it could spell life in darkness, or even death.

I say nothing, because nothing needs to be said. I cannot refuse. So instead, I take the reins from Oriane, tying them to a nearby post.

When I turn back, they've already set off into the crowd, subtly pushing their way through to the best stalls. This is one of the few times where they don't mind if it's a human or fae they'll interact with, so long as the goods are worth it. I hurry after them but keep a step behind as usual.

"Sarai says his favourite colour is blue," Oriane drawls, her voice hushed as she runs a hand across a soft fabric with a stunning sheen.

I keep my own hands clasped together, my head down, but my eyes flicker back and forth, drinking in all that they can.

Oriane goes on, "But I heard it's red."

"Well, that won't do. We can't have you turning up in some hideous colour." Zianne looks around, and her eyes land on a tall, copper-skinned guard walking by. Her gaze turns hungry. "Captain!"

The man stops, his dark eyes showing clear recognition once they land on my stepmother. I'm not at all surprised to find they are acquainted. Zianne has made a point of meeting everyone worth knowing.

"Lady Zianne," he greets, his voice gentle yet firm. "Is everything alright?"

If he were human, I'd say the captain would be in his early twenties. But nothing about his appearance could let me forget what he really is.

The fae are generally far more beautiful than humans. They seem almost sculpted, carefully crafted so as to be the most stunning creatures in existence. From the tips of their toes to the pointed ends of their ears. And the captain is no exception.

"Yes," Zianne says, a slight laugh to her words. I know it's forced, an attempt to lower the younger man's guard, but he seems not to notice. "I wonder if you might help us, for we cannot decide. What is the prince's favourite colour?"

The captain's face clears. "Silver, I believe. Though he is partial to green."

I glance down at my dark green dress made of a rough, scratchy material, and my cheeks heat at the thought of Jorai seeing me in this.

"Silver! Of course! Like the starlight."

The captain nods.

"Wonderful." Zianne claps her hands, a large smile lighting her face.

"Is your family shopping for the festival?" he inquires.

"Yes," Zianne says, her eyes already trailing to the stall that sells starlight gems. "I hope we're not being too presumptuous, but we're so excited to celebrate the prince's birthday."

"Not at all. I believe everyone will be invited," he says. "And you, young lady?"

I glance at Oriane but find her already looking at me. Her face pales with barely controlled rage. I jerk with the realisation the captain was asking me. Asking *me* about the festival.

"Oh, my youngest won't be attending, Captain," Zianne says smoothly before I can recover from the shock. "She has been unwell for some time. I'm afraid even today's trip will have her laid up for weeks."

"A shame," the captain replies, his eyes scanning me as though looking for some sign of the sickness Zianne mentions.

He doesn't have to look hard. My skin is pale from years stuck inside Zianne's home, my hair limp, and my body small and skinny. Zianne doesn't treat me with the same care as the rest of her property, although she is careful not to leave a mark on any visible skin.

His eyes linger on my rounded ears, but he says nothing to question Zianne's claim of kinship.

"Is your father enjoying his retirement?" Zianne asks, in what I can tell is a desperate attempt to move his attention away from me. My manacle may be covered, but Zianne is always infinitely aware of what I am.

But it works, as he turns back to my stepmother. The captain nods. "He's well, but it's been an adjustment."

"I'm sure." Zianne's voice is consoling. "But he must be proud that you've taken his place."

His stunning features seem to close off at the remark. "Indeed."

"Oh, but pardon me!" Zianne suddenly cries. "I have not introduced you to my daughter."

His brow crinkles, and he moves as though to correct her, but Zianne continues.

"This is Oriane," she says, gesturing to Oriane, who has been hanging onto his every word as though searching for hidden meaning. "This is Zephi, Captain of the Royal Guard."

My lips part. Zephi. The same man Jorai used to speak of? Who taught him to fight?

Captain Zephi hesitates, then gives into Zianne's forced introduction, one I'm sure by his expression that he has actually had before.

"A pleasure," he says, nodding his head in a short bow.

A lock of his black hair slides down his face, escaping the leather band keeping it tied back. My eyes remain fixed on him. I never did end up meeting him when my mother worked in the palace, but I can't help feeling a spark of warmth. A connection to my old life.

"Word has it that the prince is looking for a wife," Oriane says, stage whispering. "But he's not the only one the court ladies are talking about." She leans in. "You're not a bad catch yourself, Captain."

I feel my own cheeks heat at her remark, but to his credit the man doesn't appear at all ruffled. He merely offers her a polite smile.

"For now, I consider myself married to the job. But should the right young lady come along, I am willing to make room in my life for her."

"You are wise," Oriane says, nodding. Bile rises in my throat at the sickly sweetness of her tone. "The prince is lucky to have you."

"If you'll excuse me, ladies, I must return to my rounds."

We offer the captain a small curtsy, and I'm careful to keep my skirt close so it doesn't reveal my ankle as the man continues on his way. I watch his disappearing form. Jorai's friend.

As soon as he's out of earshot, Zianne turns to Oriane. "I wouldn't trust another word Sarai says. In the game for the prince's heart, a woman will say anything."

Oriane nods, her brow crinkling.

"Never mind, I shall return the favour." She gives a wicked grin, and the two hurry over to the stall selling starlight, both giggling quietly.

I trail after them, thinking back over every word Captain Zephi said about Jorai. But there's little I glean from his words.

Surely the prince is happy? Healthy?

It's another two hours before we return home, and my arms are weighed down by yards of fabric.

Oriane carries the small gems of starlight in the horse's saddlebags, while Zianne holds the rest of the jewellery and a mask for each of them.

There is nothing for me. I'm not worth spending a coin on. Not that I ever expected to be invited along. But I can't help but feel happy. Because today was the first I've heard about Jorai not directly from Zianne or Oriane. And it sounds like he's OK, and that he still has Zephi by his side.

And that's enough for me.

4

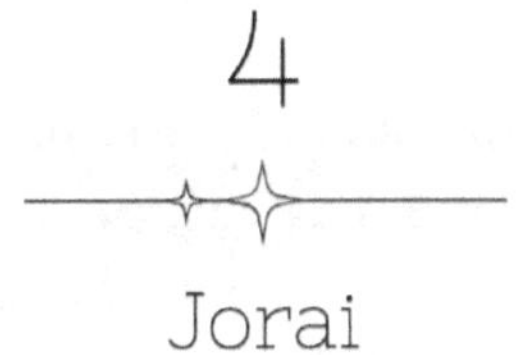

Jorai

"**G**OOD!" TAAVI PRAISES, AS the flat of my blade slaps his thigh.

I huff, easily deflecting his return blow, but the guard seems oblivious to my annoyance. Now that Zephi's father, Captain Vaile, rarely visits the palace anymore, Zephi is the only guard who will fight me properly. He's been captain since before I was born, but Vaile used to join his son regularly during my training.

"Let's change things up," I suggest, my breath hardly even laboured. Even out in the heat, with the sun shining heavily on us, I've hardly worked up a sweat.

Taavi's brow crinkles in the second before he realises what I mean.

The air grows heavy as I reach out with something deep inside myself and increase the humidity, forcing sweat to bead on our foreheads immediately. The hairs on my arms stand on end.

I twist the magic, and a light crackle fills the air as I let electricity run up and down my blade.

Taavi's eyes widen, but surprisingly he doesn't back down like many guards before him. My magic is rare, its nature meaning I appear to have control over several elements. But I rarely display my power publicly outside of my lightning. A rather helpful bluff, should I ever need it. I can control the weather in large and isolated areas.

I dive back into the fight a moment later, and our blades meet with a spark. Taavi, I know, has a small amount of water magic, passed down through his mother's line. And it's the only reason I use my own magic against him. And it's also why I increased the humidity.

But my attempt to jolt him into actually fighting me doesn't work.

In fact, he doesn't even try to use his water magic against me. Even when I weaken the electricity on my sword and tap it gently against his shoulder to give him a slight zap. Nothing.

"Come on, Taavi! I know you can fight better than this!"

"I'm sorry, Your Highness," he says, and half-heartedly flings some water in my face before sweeping low to kick out my leg. But he does it slowly. Nearly as slow as a human.

I dodge easily, and land a light punch to his abdomen, then to his jaw. But still, he does nothing.

With a sigh, I hold up my hand and drop my sword's tip to the ground. "I think we'll leave it there. Thank you, Taavi."

He doesn't try to hide his relief as he bows and hurries inside. I let go of the water in the air, of the lightning on my blade, and close my eyes, turning my face up towards the sun.

Even if Taavi had managed to hurt me, we keep healers in residence at the palace, as every guard knows from visiting after their own training sessions. Whatever damage Taavi might have done to me would not have lasted long.

And I would not have cared. I probably would have been grateful since it would have meant a proper training session, something that has been in short supply lately.

With a defeated sigh, I return my sword to its scabbard.

"Your Highness!"

"Zeph?" My eyes snap open, and I can feel a smile beginning to spread across my face. Perhaps I'll get some proper training in after all.

"The messengers have been searching for you," Zephi says, squinting as he steps down into the light. "The king has called a meeting."

My renewed excitement instantly disappears. Looks like I won't be getting that sparring match after all. "I'm coming," I sigh.

My feet sink into the soft grass as I leave the training area, jump up the three stairs, and back into an outer hall of the palace.

"How was training?" Zephi asks.

I glance at him, his deep voice betraying that he already knows the answer. I wonder whether the guards would actually listen to him this time if he spoke with them.

It's nothing against him. From what I've heard they never listened to Vaile either when it came to my father's training. I can tell he's torn between amusement and disappointment.

"You know how it went. It looks like you're stuck with me, Captain."

"Such a shame." There's a grumble of laughter to his words. Looks like the amusement won after all.

"What's this meeting about, then?"

Zephi sobers. "Frigarth."

5

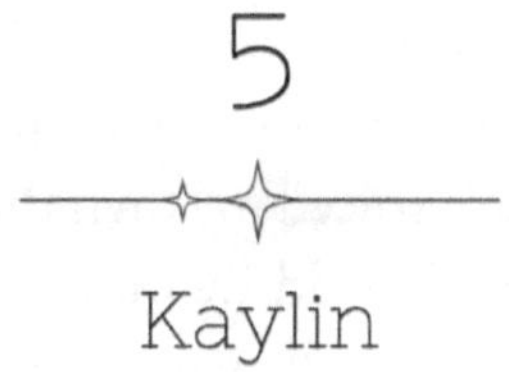

Kaylin

"WATCH IT!" ORIANE BARKS, causing me to flinch, and I narrowly avoid pricking her with the pin again.

"Sorry," I mumble, but, thankfully, her attention has left me again and I can safely return to adjusting the fabric that will become part of her dress for the first night of the festival.

The dress will be silver, of course, but with two main layers to it. This bottom layer is solid, silken, and will only cover a very small portion of her body.

Unfortunately for me, I can't try to maintain any sense of modesty or privacy as I pin the pieces in place on her. Oriane still wears her undergarments, but the fabric will cover little more than those and the space between them. Perhaps not even that if Oriane gets her way, which she usually does.

Over this will be another silver material, translucent, which will sweep down past her knees, with a split at the side to show off her legs. I'll then decorate it with the starlight gems.

It'll be a deeply revealing dress, meant to draw the prince's eye and keep it there.

I desperately hope Jorai will turn blind for his birthday.

"Oh! He'd have to be blind not to notice you!" Zianne sighs dreamily, seeing beyond the hardly-there outfit covered in pins to what she'll look like on the night. I purse my lips, realising she's voiced my own thoughts. It's a good thing she can't actually read them, though that is a gift I know for a fact she wishes she had.

Oriane giggles, pulling me from my thoughts. Satisfied with this bottom layer, I remove it, then retrieve the translucent one.

Zianne's face clouds as her eyes follow me. "I wonder why the captain seems to think the humans will be going?"

I begin to shape the fabric, positioning it over Oriane's body, pinning it as I go.

"You don't think they could actually be *invited?* I want that lower, Kaylin."

I adjust the fabric to reveal more of her chest. My stepmother is silent for a long moment.

"Mother?" Oriane demands.

"I believe ... they might be."

My stepsister splutters, "Why?"

"Frigarth," Zianne says simply. And it's enough.

Because the rumour is that the slavery of humans was only outlawed to secure friendship with Frigarth—our neighbour to the North with a mixed court of humans and fae. Ashennor was, and is, in desperate need of an ally in case Ellcombe, unsatisfied with its current conquests, turns its greedy sights to us.

It was a rumour only whispered among my people when I still lived with them, but many of the fae believe it's true.

My stepsister scoffs. "We don't need them! What use is a weak, vermin-loving country to us?"

"And yet, I don't think the king will change his mind without a little incentive." Zianne gives her a wide smile.

Oriane's face clears, but her eyes flicker to me. I don't acknowledge her gaze, fleeting as it is, but keep my gaze on her dress.

"That could be fun," she finally says. Something in her voice makes me shiver, but her tone lightens. "Could you imagine our little Kaylin going?" She laughs. "Will you decorate your manacle with starlight to hide what you are? Pity nothing will wipe the stench from you."

"Not even the soot would rise from your skin anymore. You're so filthy, Kaylin," Zianne's voice rings with a mix of humour and disgust.

"Yes, Stepmother," I say, used to their biting remarks.

I finish my work in silence, and hurry to my chores as soon as I'm dismissed. I'm still expected to complete my usual jobs even though I've spent hours with Zianne and Oriane at the markets and then in getting their dresses ready.

Zianne insists on a clean home, something that is virtually impossible with its open plan, but I'm to succeed anyway. As I sweep the house, going from room to room, I find myself humming a tune my mother used to sing while she worked in the palace. I grin. It was hard to find a moment when she *wasn't* singing. She said it made the work more fun.

I can scarcely remember the lyrics of this one, but I'm certain the tune will never leave me. It's like a familiar embrace. A touch on the shoulder. A reminder of her.

For a moment, I can almost hear her sweet voice rising to join mine. It drowns out the sting of Oriane and Zianne's wicked laughter.

I move from tune to tune and room to room, sometimes humming, sometimes singing a remembered lyric. My stepmother says nothing of it. It is one of the few exceptions to her rule of never being noticed. Zianne has a soft spot for music.

Once, I swear I heard her hum a line too, but I could never be certain. I mop next, and then it's into the kitchen. The cupboards are due for a full and deep clean, as is the sink.

When it's time for dinner, Zianne and Oriane are louder than usual. Happily chatting and laughing and planning what they'll do and say at the festival. They unpack every idea, every scheme to get Jorai's attention and, most importantly, his heart.

Not once does Oriane profess any semblance of love for him. Not once does she express any interest in *him*. They couldn't be clearer that this match is all for the crown.

But I don't say anything. My opinion doesn't matter. My words would mean nothing.

So, I keep silent while I listen from the kitchen floor, eating bread and sweet cheese. Even when they relive their conversation with Captain Zephi and fall in raucous laughter at the idea of me attending in my soot-covered dress.

And then it's more cleaning. My life doesn't hold much variety.

By the time the lock clicks behind me as I crawl into bed exhausted, the night is dark and my room is as cold as ever. But as I pull my thread-bare blanket close, I can't help but picture what it would be like going to the festival.

Dancing under the stars in a silver dress. Glimpsing Jory again.

Would he even recognise me now?

The girl he knew back then was a totally different person, inside and out, compared to the one I am now. I took everything for granted as a young girl. The friends I had. The family. The freedom.

But in my mind, his eyes find mine, and he smiles.

6

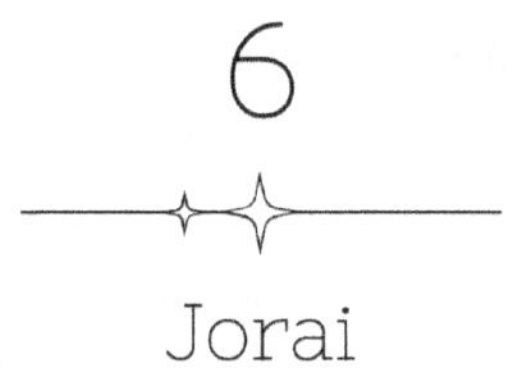

Jorai

"F RIGARTH?" I FROWN, LOOKING across at Zephi.

"That's not all. The rebels have issued another threat."

My heart sinks.

"Bad?"

"It is not good, Your Highness." He hesitates as though there's more he wants to say, but he's not sure of me.

"Go ahead, Zeph."

"You cannot allow your father to change his mind about the humans, in any capacity. Even with attending the festival. Not with Frigarth so on edge."

I nod, and I can tell he's relieved that I agree, though he does well in trying to hide it. If we did not have such a strong friendship, I probably wouldn't have noticed. Not many do with his emotions. He's usually a closed book.

"I know," I say, mentally preparing myself. "My father will understand."

"If you remind him of all that would be lost, I believe he will."

I swallow. Yes, he will. But Zephi is right. I will have to speak up and risk my father's displeasure, however brief. I square my shoulders.

It needs to be done. For the good of Ashennor.

My father is waiting for us in his office, my Aunt Cyra sitting opposite him.

I stifle a laugh at the realisation that she's brought in her own chair, her wild curly hair just visible over the high, thickly cushioned back.

"Jorai!" She jumps to her feet as she catches sight of me and throws her arms around me, pulling me in for a tight embrace.

Cyra is short for a fae, nearly a full foot shorter than me, but it all adds to her image. Her bubbly, slightly air-brained, crazy-haired image. She's woven a crown of flowers into her hair today, no doubt using her magic to summon them and keep them from wilting.

I return the hug with a soft smile. Cyra is one of my favourite people in all of Ashennor.

The king clears his throat.

"Yes, yes," Cyra says, pulling back from me, but then she launches herself at Zephi. "How are you, Captain? You're looking well." She makes a show of looking him over as she often does with me, turning him this way and that.

"Very well, my lady." He offers her a polite nod.

"Still keeping to the titles, I see," Cyra playfully chides. "At least you've dropped highness."

"Yes, my lady."

"Cy," my father sighs, pinching his nose.

With a laugh, Cyra, his sister, returns to her chair. "Alright then, go ahead, Eran."

He waits until Zephi and I are seated, our backs inches away from the hard wood of the chairs.

"The rebels wish to attend Jorai's birthday celebrations," he finally says bitterly, brandishing a piece of paper.

"Fair enough," Cyra says, lightly, "I imagine everyone wishes to come! But I assume they don't want to dance?"

My father rolls his eyes, a reaction only she can seem to get out of him.

"What do they want?" I ask, but I already know. It always comes back to the same thing. The humans back where they used to be. In slavery.

"Reinstatement, of course. But they've heard word that you're inviting the humans to your birthday. They're willing to start with the invitations being halted."

Zephi shifts beside me.

I pause, letting it seem as though I'm thinking furiously, though I've already made up my mind. I just hope he'll listen.

"So, we'll increase the presence of the guards. Make sure the rebels can't possibly cause trouble for the humans attending."

My father looks at me shrewdly but says nothing of my suggestion for the moment.

"We have also received word from Frigarth. They're sending an ambassador."

"Oh, who's coming?" Cyra chimes, her eyes alight, but I can tell she's hanging on my father's every word. Sometimes I wonder ...

"He hasn't been here before." He glances down at a roll of parchment. "Raiden somebody. He'll arrive any day now."

My eyebrow rises. For the ambassador to be nearly here already, my father must have known for weeks. These kinds of things never happen overnight.

"Then we can't afford to back down on the humans, not with Frigarth watching so closely."

The paper still clutched in his hand crumples, and a shadow passes over his face. "They have no right to demand this of me!"

I'm not sure who 'they' are but, knowing my father, he means both the rebels and Frigarth. But since they're on opposing sides, he'll have to meet one of them at least halfway.

"I know, I know," Cyra says, waving her hand airily. "Who knew ruling a country was so political?"

The king's eyes narrow, but he remains silent.

Cyra's voice, however, hardens ever so slightly. "Yet here we are, Eran. And these decisions have already been made. You chose Frigarth. You hardly need us here to tell you that."

"Father," I say, pressing the advantage Cyra has given me, "we can't give in to the rebels. They'll only demand more, and we'll lose our only ally against Ellcombe."

"I know," he bites out.

Zephi finally speaks. "I can assign another squad to the festival, Your Majesty." He tilts his head. "Perhaps even a few of the new recruits; it would be good experience for them."

It's a long moment before my father finally speaks, and he's managed to regain some of his composure once he does. "Very well. I want two extra squads, Captain. Bring along as many recruits as you feel necessary. No need to pass up a good opportunity for them."

Zephi nods a bow.

"And what about this ambassador?" I ask, my eyes drawn to the parchment on the desk, but I can't make anything out from where I'm sitting.

"You're to keep him company, Jorai. I don't want him hanging onto me every moment of the day. We'll organise a formal meeting when he arrives, but you're to see that he's satisfied."

"Very well." I need to learn all I can about this Raiden, preferably before he arrives. But it shouldn't be too difficult to keep him happy.

After all, the rumours circulating Ashennor are only that. Rumours. The rebels might make threats, but it doesn't change the fact that the humans are better treated today than ever before. The fact that their population has boomed is proof enough. And I'll make sure Ambassador Raiden sees that.

"What can I do?" Cyra asks, tucking a length of her hair back from her face.

"I'm sure you already have plans to *investigate* the ambassador."

It's a low blow, and an insubstantial one. Cyra loves people. Simply adores them. She just has to introduce herself to everyone she meets and learn everything about them. It's just who she is and, I suspect, may also have a political motivation behind it as well.

But she never takes it further than that. She's never shown that kind of interest in anyone since Gaara, the uncle I never knew.

"Father," I chide. He used to be a kinder man, at least amongst the fae, I've been told. Before I was born. Before he lost *her*. My mother. These two, though siblings, have had such different responses to losing their loved ones. Ones that I never met.

"No matter, Jorai." She waves her hand again, but her voice now carries a hint of strain. "He's been thankful for my friendships before. I'm sure he will be again."

She leaves without waiting for his dismissal. One of the guards hurries in to remove her chair.

"Have a room made up for the ambassador," my father says, his ice-blue eyes locking on mine. "Make sure it overlooks the city."

"Cyra!" I hurry to catch up with my aunt, catching a glimpse of the hem of her blue dress as she turns a corner. Her head reappears, frowning until she sees me.

"Jorai?"

I don't say anything until I've joined her, and we continue through the open halls.

"Do you know anything about this new ambassador?" Cyra is a wealth of information, and I'd be remiss to ignore her.

Her eyes sparkle as she glances at me. "A little."

"And could you be persuaded to share with your favourite nephew?"

She laughs. "You're my only nephew! But when have I ever managed to deny you anything?"

I grin. This is the game we always play. And though it's childish, I can't resist it.

"I don't know much," she admits, her pace never wavering as she winds back through the palace. "But I can tell you he used to be a soldier. A palace guard in Frigarth, seventeen years ago." She draws out this last sentence.

I stumble. "He was there when Princess Zara disappeared? How did he become an ambassador then?"

Cyra nods approvingly. "He spent the next fifteen years looking for her. And he only retired from service when he was injured in a skirmish. But word is, being an ambassador is just another attempt to find her."

"But I thought all the guards on duty were dismissed?"

"They were," she says, her expression turning thoughtful. "But they trust Raiden implicitly. I'd dearly love to find out why."

"Maybe you'll get your chance," I say, determined to give it to her. Any man who can go through all that and still remain in the favour of royalty is a man worth meeting. And Cyra can get anything out of anyone.

7

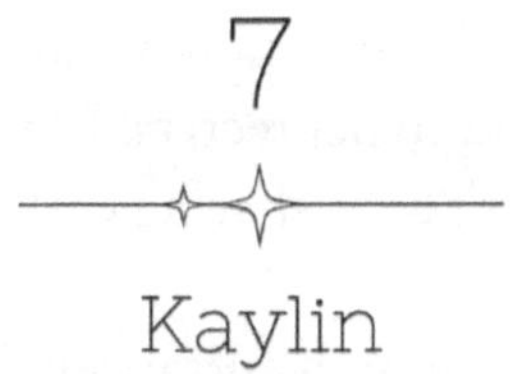

Kaylin

Z IANNE KEEPS UP A relentless schedule over the next
few days, but I don't know what I'm being punished
for this time. I think back over our every encounter, every
word since the day we went to the markets, as I scrub every
inch of the estate, but nothing stands out.

Perhaps I was short with her? Or I said something I
shouldn't have? I'm sure I've done something to deserve
this, but what?

I take the punishment quietly and merely focus on getting everything done. I've still got to work on Oriane and
Zianne's dresses for the festival, as well. But once we find

out how many days the celebrations will last for, I'll have to make them more. One dress for each day.

Selfishly, I hope it'll all be over quickly. But that's not how the fae celebrate. Especially the royals.

But I shouldn't think like that. It's Jorai's birthday; it could go for a week, and no one would mind. In fact, people would be disappointed it didn't last longer. So, I shouldn't complain.

There's a soft knock at the front entrance, and Sarai's voice calls through the house. "Oriane!"

I hurry to greet her, tugging at my hem to hide my ankle. Sarai wouldn't care if she knew what I was, but Zianne doesn't trust her to keep her secrets. Especially not with the false information she's been sharing with Oriane about Jorai and the party.

I curtsy as I reach the arch entranceway to the house, but Sarai is already stepping inside. Her brown hair is pulled up into a braided crown today, a long silver chain platted through it, the ends dangling down behind her pointed ears.

She's not quite as beautiful as Oriane, but if my step-sister's gossip is to be believed, she's still received quite the amount of interest from court men.

But her eyes, like every other woman's, are set on the prince. Or rather, the crown.

"Welcome, my lady," I say, though Sarai has no official title or position. "Can I take your—"

A strong shove from behind sends me reeling into a pillar as Oriane appears, floating forwards as if she never saw me. I can't tell if she's used her magic or physically pushed me;

neither would come as a surprise. I manage to regain my balance and turn my eyes down, waiting for a command. My back tingles, the skin already tender.

"Sarai! Oh, I have so much to tell you!" Oriane exclaims, delicately kissing Sarai's tanned cheek. Sarai returns the gesture, her emerald eyes lighting up hungrily.

"Do tell, Ori, I'm dying for any morsel of gossip." And with that, the two sweep off, leaving me unnoticed by the entrance.

As they leave, I hear Oriane drawl, "Well, guess who we ran into at the markets?"

No doubt Oriane will tell Sarai the prince's favourite colour, as heard from the Captain of the Royal Guard himself, is mustard yellow. My lips twitch at their silliness as I practically run back to the kitchen. Any second now, they'll ask for refreshments.

I'm already carrying a tray of iced tea, delicate loi berries, and sweet apple, when the summons comes. They're in Oriane's room already waiting for me.

Pushing through the soft, translucent curtain, I duck inside, carefully balancing the tray as I cross to the small table they sit by. Oriane's room is easily as large as the living area closest to the dining room. Her bed—humungous and covered in pillows and drapes—is set to the left, the engraved head against the wall.

Directly opposite the entrance is her wardrobe, spanning nearly half the entire back wall with gems of starlight dotted across it. And to the right is the sitting area, where Oriane and Sarai now sit in two large, cushioned chairs on either side of a rounded table.

"There you are, Kaylin. I was beginning to think you'd gone deaf," Oriane says snidely, a glint in her eyes as I serve their food and drink. Sarai giggles.

"I'm sorry, Oriane. I will be quicker next time."

She turns her nose up. "Indeed, you will."

"Can you believe what they're saying about the festival?" Sarai says, her hard eyes travelling over me from my hair down to my bare feet. "That the humans might be invited?"

Oriane scoffs, waving me away as she reaches for her glass.

"I hear he may have been convinced to see reason. The prince isn't foolish enough to anger his people ..." Her voice fades as I wander back to the kitchen.

But their words mean little to me. I wouldn't have been invited anyway.

As a slave, I'm even less than human.

Two days later, the key in my door twists, and I hurry upstairs to prepare breakfast as usual. Zianne says nothing to hurry me along, looking out over the back garden.

I wince. I ran out of daylight to work in the garden yesterday, and Zianne has a gift for spotting weeds. But when I come back with her breakfast, there is the very hint of a smile on her face as I serve her. It bursts into life when Oriane appears.

"Good morning, my dear." She gestures to the seat opposite her and leans forwards as Oriane takes it. "My friend was kind enough to inform me that today is the day."

Oriane's face shines just as brightly as her mother's. "The invitations?" she whispers with false question.

"Indeed."

The two giggle as they pick at their meals, both practically glowing with excitement. Zianne's *friend* has been a big source of information for years now.

"Braid my hair back, Kaylin. It's getting in the way." Zianne's voice is lighter than it has been all week.

If this mood lasts, today will be a good day.

The invitations arrive within the hour, a light trumpet announcing the royal messenger. But surprisingly, Zianne sends me to greet them.

"We mustn't appear too eager," she says to Oriane as I hurry along, even though she's changed into one of her favourite dresses and had me redo her hair.

The human man, dressed in a black and gold tunic, hands me a large envelope.

"There will be no need to respond," he explains, his deep voice already exhausted. It seems the man has had quite a long morning. The festival is only next week, which means he must get all the invitations out as quickly as possible.

He disappears down the path to the next estate with barely a word.

I stare at the envelope in my hands and come back inside. It glistens with a delicate silver-white dust. Starlight. Just how much of it does the royal family have?

"It's the invitations," I say, holding it out for Zianne.

She snatches it from my hands, all pretence of indifference gone. She tears it open with long painted nails and pulls a single, thick sheet of silver parchment from within. Her eyes scan it, but by the time she reaches the end, every sign of happiness, of excitement, is gone.

"What is it, Mother?" Oriane says, leaving her chair and reading over Zianne's shoulder. Her face turns a deep purplish-red.

I take an involuntary step backwards. It's never a good idea to be around when Oriane goes into a rage. And it looks like one is brewing.

But I haven't been dismissed. I wring my hands in my skirt.

"That—! How dare—! As if we'd—!" Oriane splutters, her features twisting. Perhaps they weren't invited? But that would be the biggest snub of the century. Of several centuries.

But then her eyes land on me.

"You!" Oriane screams, launching herself across the room.

Her hands are in my hair in seconds, tugging my head sideways as she screeches wordlessly at me. She drags her long nails down my neck.

"Oriane! Contain yourself." Zianne has risen to her feet.

A move that is enough to halt the nails still at my throat. A bead of something warm trickles under my collar. And I know that it is only this, the visibility of such an injury, that has made Zianne step in.

"Now really," Zianne says, her mouth twisting into a smile, "Who are we to stop Kaylin from attending?"

My mouth drops open.

"I—I'm invited?" My voice is strained, but I can't keep the hope from mingling with the surprise in my voice.

"Indeed." Zianne holds out the invitation for me, and Oriane finally releases my hair. I'm sure she's taken more than a few strands with her judging from the pain in my scalp.

But there's no denying it as I stare down at the paper. There's my initial underneath Zianne and Oriane's names. Their last name tacked onto mine in accordance with my adoption. And signed at the bottom ... is Captain Zephi.

My heart jumps and stutters. The captain made sure I was invited, despite being told I was too sick to attend? I doubt my full name is listed in Zianne's records, as adoption is an easy process in Ashennor given the lack of fae births and high fae maternity deaths.

But the captain must have found something, however small.

"I—I'm invited?" I splutter in shock.

"Yes, stupid girl!" Zianne snaps, snatching the paper back. "And if you are to attend then there are just a few prerequisites. All your jobs are to be completed to the best of your ability, not rushed, do you hear me?"

I nod, a tentative smile beginning to tug at my face.

"You're to make your own dress and it must be new. I won't have you arriving in rags."

I nod again. This will be difficult, but I'm sure I can scrape something together from left-over material from dresses I've made for them in the past.

Oriane's mouth has dropped open and she stands silent, glancing between us in disbelief.

"And you are to be on your best behaviour. I will revoke your invitation the second you speak back to me. Understood?" Something dark clings to her face as she smiles, but I can't bring myself to worry.

Jory. I'm going to see Jory again.

"Yes. Yes, thank you, Stepmother!"

With a scream of rage, Oriane trumps from the room. But I'll worry about her moods later.

Right now, nothing could possibly bring me down.

8

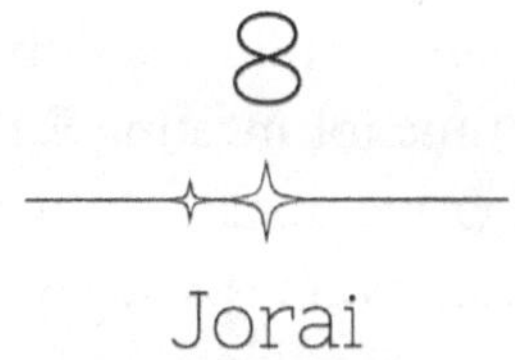

Jorai

*T*HERE'S NO NEED TO *be nervous,* I tell myself over and over. *We have nothing to hide. Nothing to be concerned about.*

Raiden will find nothing to worry Frigarth during his visit. *There's no need to be nervous.*

I catch myself before saying it out loud as I walk into my office, taking a seat opposite Zephi and Cyra at my desk. "Any news?" I ask.

"The ambassador will be here within the hour," Zephi says, his face betraying nothing. But surely my friend is concerned—he's been in my ear for days about the humans.

Cyra bounces in her seat. "Oh, good! I can't wait to get my first look at the ambassador."

This draws a smile from me. Even Zephi's lips twitch, and Cyra winks.

"We have nothing to hide," I say, more for Zephi than for me now. "He'll be headed home before we know it."

Zephi purses his lips. "I hope you're right, Your Highness."

But it's clear he's still not happy. What more does he want? The humans are coming to the festival, they're equal. There are no slaves, despite whatever whispers he's heard.

We go over our plans. I still haven't been able to get my father to confirm a time for meeting Raiden himself. I get the feeling that he'd rather not see the man at all.

It feels like only seconds have passed when there is a knock at the door.

Taavi pokes his head inside. "He's arrived, Your Highness."

Ambassador Raiden looks more like a warrior than an ambassador, and suddenly I'm glad for Cyra's information. Dressed from head to toe in leather, every inch of his exposed skin a deep tan from years in the sun, and two swords strapped across his back, he doesn't try to hide his past.

Raiden is perhaps two inches shorter than me, with hair so light it appears almost white. His shoulders are broad, and his muscled physique puts even Zephi to shame. Though, I'm sure they are around the same age.

There's no sign of whatever injury led to his change in career. His eyes are curious, kind even, as he returns my studying look. I wonder what he sees.

"Welcome to Ashennor, Ambassador," I say, crossing the short distance between us and holding out my hand.

The fae man shakes it, his grip firm, and smiles. "A pleasure, Prince Jorai. Your country is beautiful. King Turin sends his greetings."

"I hope he is well. It's been some time since we last saw him."

Cyra delicately clears her throat.

I supress a laugh. "This is my aunt, Cyra. I'm afraid she's heard rumours about you, Ambassador, and has been keen to meet you."

She subtly elbows me as she passes. "Raiden, is it?"

"Yes, Your Highness," he says.

"A pleasure."

"I'm sure it's all mine." He winks. *Winks* at my aunt.

But she merely laughs as though he's said something funny. As though they've traded some kind of inside joke. "Oh no, it's definitely mine."

"Come inside, I'll show you to your room." I've never been able to work out Cyra's games, but I'm not sure about leaving her to it right now.

"Thank you, I'll be glad to get rid of this bag," he says, tugging at the strap over his shoulder.

The ambassador came alone. A rare and brave move, not that he has anything to fear from us. It'll be Ashennor that comes out poorly from this visit, if anyone.

"You'll be staying just down the hall from me," I say, leading him back inside the palace. Cyra falls in step beside us, while Zephi silently brings up the rear.

"I am honoured."

"My father sends his apologies for not being here to greet you. Unfortunately, he's been delayed by some work. Hopefully, he'll be able to join us for dinner."

"I understand, Your Highness." Something in his voice tells me he understands much more than I've said. And I'm thankful he doesn't challenge me about my father's whereabouts. I wouldn't know where he is anyway.

"I'm told this is your first time in Ashennor?" I prompt.

"Ahh," he says. "I've not been to your capital, but I have travelled through your country before. I'm glad to be able to stop and see it properly."

"I'm sure you'll enjoy your stay. With the festival coming, the city is full to bursting and preparations are well underway."

He nods. "I look forward to it. I enjoy a good party."

I study Raiden from the corner of my eye as I lead him through the halls. His words are formal, chosen more to feel me out than anything else.

He's trying to get a read of me, the same way I am with him. So, what can I tell from this brief encounter? Not much. Other than I suspect he may actually have a sense of humour under there.

But he is also surprisingly friendly for an ambassador. His tone and words have been chosen to convey friendship and openness rather than the typical stuffiness associated with his position.

Working with him may not actually be too bad.

"Oh, so do I," Cyra trills. "Can I count on a dance during the festivities, Ambassador? I've managed to wrangle one from Captain Zephi, as well."

"Of course, my lady. I'd be a fool to turn a beauty such as yourself down," he says with a rogue smile.

There it is. A hint of himself shining through. And Cyra drew it out within minutes of his arrival.

My aunt laughs. "Ambassador, indeed."

Their shameless flirting would probably bother me if they seemed closer in age. But I find myself smothering a grin at his smooth talk. Liking Cyra is hardly a test of anyone—you'd be hard-pressed to find someone who doesn't love her—but I find myself warming to Raiden.

"Here we are." I stop outside one of the rooms, finding a light curtain has been hung across the entranceway as a token of privacy. I can count on one hand the number of doors we have here in the palace. I don't go inside, instead letting Raiden lead the way.

He glances around, taking in the large bed, desk, wardrobe, and bathing facilities.

The room looks out over the eastern side of the city, but there is a strip of well-kept flowers in between that leads to the main gardens off to our right. It's a fine view, giving the bedroom a peaceful air to it.

Raiden nods. "Thank you."

"I'm sure you'd like to freshen up before lunch. We'll come to collect you soon, and then I'll show you around properly afterwards."

We duck out of the room, with Cyra throwing him a smile over her shoulder. I don't ask Zephi to post anyone outside his room. We have nothing to hide. The ambassador is welcome to wander around the palace, and the guards will stop him from entering anywhere he, or anyone else, shouldn't.

·)⟩➤●❰❰(·

"How was your journey, Ambassador Raiden? Forgive us, but I believe in the excitement of your arrival we forgot to ask," Cyra says, smiling as she takes a sip from her glass. I resist the urge to grimace. I *had* forgotten to ask.

But Raiden simply smiles. "Please, just call be Raiden. I've never been one for titles."

Interesting, since he's been careful to use mine.

"It was a rather uneventful trip," he continues, pausing to take a bite of the delicate pastry served for lunch. "But I rather enjoyed it once I crossed the border."

My lips curve upwards. I can't even begin to think of the kind of political disaster that would have occurred if something had happened to him in our lands. He might be able to handle himself, but he really should have brought some guards.

"How did you find our outer towns?" I ask, gently prodding. The sooner I can gauge his thoughts on Ashennor and these rumours, the sooner I can work out how to keep him and Frigarth happy. Raiden doesn't make me wait.

He frowns. "I didn't get to stay in them nearly as long as I would have liked. King Turin and I are very concerned with the whispers circulating."

"Whispers?" I press, my hand slowly closing around a pitcher of juice.

His blue eyes meet mine. "Of the mistreatment of humans. I didn't witness anything myself; I can't say that I stayed anywhere long enough in order to do so."

I let his words hang in the air, taking a swig of my drink. If I respond too quickly, it would appear as though I'm trying to hide something. Which I most definitely am not. I wonder if the ambassador is aware of the subtleties of politics.

"There is nothing to be concerned about, Raiden. These whispers are nothing more than a few old-fashioned fae wishing to cause us trouble. I assure you, the humans in Ashennor are treated exactly like the rest of our people."

He cocks his head. "I would be happy to see it."

"I'm sure you will." I smile, and it's only half forced. "I'd be honoured if you attended the celebrations for my birthday next week. Humans and fae will both be in attendance, of course, and it'll be the perfect time to see our people in harmony together."

"Be careful what you say, Ambassador," Cyra chides, her tone teasing, and I feel the mood instantly lighten. "You've already accepted a dance with me."

"And I would no sooner turn down my Queen Laurel!" He grins, sitting back in his chair. "Indeed, it's been much too long since I went to a party."

I find myself thankful that Zephi wasn't able to attend this small lunch. He's not a man of many words, but I can't have him sharing his own concerns with the ambassador. The last thing I need is for my captain to give him the wrong idea. A stab of guilt hits me at the thought. But my country can't afford for this visit to go poorly. I'm lucky to have Cyra with me.

"Oh, dear Laurel!" Cyra touches her hand to her heart, but her smile trembles. Gaara was Laurel's younger brother. "How is she?" my aunt asks.

"She is well." Raiden bobs his head. "The queen has started a new initiative among fae women. Birthing is so rare among our kind and so dangerous, as you know," he says gently, "and Her Majesty wished to help. She's been involved in health-care from what I've heard. She's flourishing."

I can't say anything for a full minute, because I do know. My own mother died just days after having me. Our kind have so few children, some couples even choosing not to have any, because of the risk involved.

It's one of the reasons humans were so popular as slaves and still are in Ellcombe. Their ease of having children means there are many of them.

"How wonderful! I can see how that would suit her."

Indeed, losing Zara—her own infant daughter—whether to death or some other fate, would have been hard for the Queen of Frigarth. Cyra was careful not to say that, but even Raiden seems to understand what she meant.

A shadow crosses his face, and I get a glimpse of the warrior within. "Yes, indeed."

A glance at Cyra shows that like me, she's realised now is not the right time to ask about the missing princess or Raiden's involvement.

"How about a trip down to the markets tomorrow, Raiden?" Cyra asks, her eyes flicking to mine, an open question in them.

I nod. "We don't have any plans for tomorrow. It'd be a great opportunity to get a taste of Ashennor."

He instantly perks up. "If there's food, I'm sold."

His comment takes me by surprise, and I laugh. "Not quite what I meant, but there will be food."

We finish the meal with light, meaningless conversation, but my spirits have lifted. Things are going better than I expected.

9

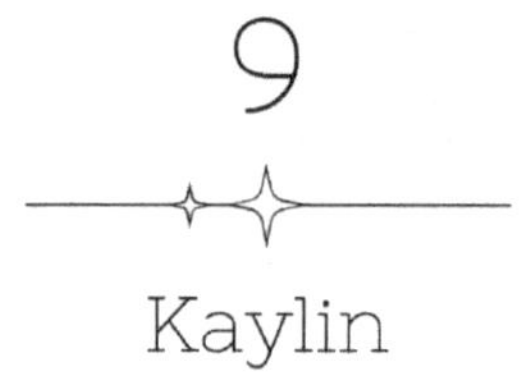

Kaylin

THE NEXT MORNING, I start on my dress. Last night I had laid out some strips of fabric, using the dim light shining under my door to find them. When it had grown too dark, I had gone from touch alone, too excited to wait for the morning. Now I can fully see what I chose.

A mix of purples, light and dark, from several of the more day-to-day dresses I've made for Orianne and Zianne over the years are laid out on a crate of potatoes. I didn't dare pick from their more expensive tastes—though, that fabric is kept in my workroom anyway. They'd be sure to miss it. But these will do me just fine. It's already better than anything I've ever worn.

I lay the pieces, two large squares of violet and fuchsia, and one small, beaded strip of light purple, on my bed, and step back to look them over with a decisive nod.

The problem will be making sure I have enough to hide my scarred ankles. The scar on the inner side of my arm from the blood bond is hardly even noteworthy, and I don't have enough fabric to cover that anyway. I doubt anyone would think it more than a simple wound.

"I'm going to the festival," I murmur. Then, for good measure, I say it again.

I've done nothing more than stare at the fabric, mentally playing around with the material, when the key turns and I run upstairs to start the day.

Zianne doesn't acknowledge me as I serve her, and only offers a mere wave of the hand to dismiss me. Oriane is nowhere to be seen, so I take that as my cue to go to her. I'd rather risk her wrath for trying to serve her than for not.

Peeking through her curtain reveals her to be sitting up in bed, a silky gown wrapped around her shoulders, a book in her hands. I frown. Oriane usually scorns books. But I duck inside anyway, bringing a tray with me.

Her grey eyes rise to mine, rage boils inside them even though her face is blank.

"I thought you had forgotten me," she says stiffly as I place the tray on her lap.

"Of course not, sister," I say, bustling around the room. I don't dare explain that I'd served her mother first. Excuses don't mean anything.

I chance a glance her way and make out the writing on the cover of her book. It's a journal. The very same she boasts contains the wealth of gossip she's collected over the years, no doubt. I hurry to drop my eyes before she notices.

I'm not technically supposed to know about it, because Oriane had been pretending I wasn't there when she'd mentioned it to her mother. Acknowledging it now would be foolish, particularly since she still seems to be in a bad mood from yesterday.

"Can I get you anything else?" I inquire.

She sniffs. "I want you to work on my dresses today. Especially the second one, as it might be my last chance to impress Jorai."

I frown. The festival is meant to be three days, but I don't risk her ire by correcting her. "Of course. We'll start as soon as you're ready."

"We will," she says, then in perfect imitation of her mother, waves me off.

Oriane's second dress will be white instead, and I have some ideas for the design. Even if I'd rather she go in a sack. I stifle a gasp at the rebellious thought as I walk back to the kitchen. But I can't help it.

Her pursuit, and every other girl's, of Jorai bothers me. I just can't help it. The kind young boy I knew as a child deserves someone who'll love him.

I can't pull my thoughts into line until I nearly send the dessert bread I've left sitting for tonight off the edge of the kitchen bench.

"Kaylin," I whisper-admonish myself. "Pull yourself together. It's not your place to worry about him."

"What are you talking about in there?"

I nearly jump through the roof.

"Just planning my day, Stepmother," I call, wincing. Fae hearing is a tricky thing sometimes. Depending on where Zianne is at the table, she can hear me from most places in the kitchen. I'd just assumed she had moved into the sitting room but, thinking back, I didn't even check earlier.

Swallowing, I take a calming breath. Everything will be fine.

I spend the whole day working with Oriane on her dresses, mainly her first one despite her demands, and it's the biggest test on my restraint that I've had in a long time. Whatever has gotten into me today had better be gone by tomorrow.

I can't afford to slip up when Zianne could revoke my invitation.

"No, no, no!" Oriane tugs the train of her dress from my hands. "It's not sitting right!"

"It's the weight of the starlight gems," I say, calmly pointing to the culprits she'd insisted I add. "They're too heavy for the skirt. It needs some of the lighter ones; these would do better along your chest."

I can see her mind working, the desire to scold me at war with the desire to look better than everyone else. "Well, why didn't you do that in the first place? Hurry up and fix it."

I guess both won out. Nonetheless, I say, "You're right."

I help her out of the dress, then gently spread it out over the table I moved into the room earlier today. We're in my usual working room, where I make all their custom clothes. The walls are lined with fabrics, ribbons, buttons, and all kinds of other embellishments.

It might be another job I have to do for them, but this is my favourite one. It reminds me of my mother, and the time I used to spend with her while she made clothes for herself and sometimes for my godmother.

A pang of longing for them both hits me. Though my godmother is alive, she may as well be on the other side of the world. Zianne can see to it that we will never cross paths so long as she's around.

It takes an hour of work to rearrange the gems, then work new ones into the upper layer of material at the bust of the dress. But it looks so much better.

Oriane insists on trying it on again.

She squeals. "Oh, Sarai is just going to die when she sees this."

I nod along, sticking pins in here and there as I circle her. "It's nearly done. We'll be able to work on the one for the third night soon."

"Did you save some of those gems for my hair?" She tosses a sheet of it over her shoulder as though to emphasise the point.

"Yes." I point, a pin still in my hand, to a small pile on the table.

"Good, I want to look like a princess when Jorai sees me."

"You will." Somehow, I manage to sound like my usual self. I'm impressed.

Oriane sighs, fiddling with the fabric of her skirt as she looks into a floor-to-ceiling mirror. "I'm so glad you work for us, Kaylin. This dress ..." Her eyes soften, and for a moment she truly is beautiful.

"Thank you, Oriane."

The moment passes, and she turns to look down her nose at me. "I hope you have something even better than this for my other dress. It has to look fae-made, after all."

A silent nod is my only response as I finish my alterations.

"Kaylin, come."

Zianne's voice is quiet, but it carries clearly through the house so that I know she's used her magic to push it along a current of air towards me.

I gently lower the beginnings of my dress onto my bed and follow her voice back upstairs.

Zianne is outside lying delicately on a lounge chair that overlooks the back garden during the day. Tonight, she is watching the myriad of stars twinkle overhead. A blue silk wrap is around her shoulders, but the air is still warm.

I stop beside her.

"What are you doing down in that root cellar?" she asks curtly.

My bedroom has many names depending on her mood.

"I'm working on my dress, Stepmother."

Her face seems to freeze, but when I blink, the stiffness is gone and she smiles at me. "Oh, how nice. How are our dresses coming along?"

"They'll be ready in time. I should have Oriane's second done tomorrow."

"Well, why aren't you working on it right now?" Her tone is even, and her eyes flick back to the stars.

"But—" I bite my cheek. "I'll get right onto it."

She nods. "Good."

I follow her eyes up to the sky. The fae might be known for their love of nature, but as I look up at the silver lights twinkling so far away, I feel an inexplicable pull.

The world seems free and infinite at night. Like if I reached up, I could be swept away.

"Kaylin?"

"Sorry." I offer her a small curtsy, then duck back inside to my work room.

·)➤●◄(·

With just two days until the festival Zianne pulls me from my work. My load has increased double, and yet I'm still expected to manage it all perfectly. A glance in the mirror in the fabric room this morning revealed large bags under bloodshot eyes. Despite all the work, my dress is now half done. But my shoulders begin to droop at the thought of whatever job Zianne has now conjured up.

"Oriane and I are having guests tonight, Kaylin, and I want everything to be perfect." Stepmother looks me up and down, wrinkling her nose. "You'll be serving the meal. You are not to speak, not to look anyone in the eye. Wear your brown dress and the apron."

I feel the familiar tingling through my body, through my blood, and shiver.

Twice in a week? The command will have worn out by the time these people arrive, but the warning is clear enough. I am not to screw up.

I give a firm nod.

"This is what you're to have ready by the time they arrive."

She hands me a list, and I feel my eyes widen. This will take all day to prepare. Whoever they've invited must be important, or at least important to impress.

"Is there something wrong?" Her voice carries a warning note.

"No, Stepmother."

"Good. Now, go." She gives me her signature wave-off.

I hurry into the kitchen. It's not until I'm there that I realise, my brown dress doesn't cover my ankles.

10

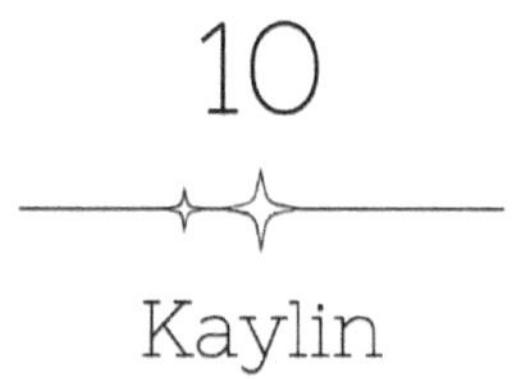

Kaylin

THERE'S A KNOCK BY the house entranceway, and I push back a strand of hair from my sweaty face with a sigh. It can't be time already, can it?

I strain my ears, struggling to hear over the spitting and hissing of the cooking meal that Zianne has ordered.

"Faina! Oh, how good to see you. We missed you at our last gathering."

Gathering? I frown but dismiss this as a simple quirk of wording. Surely, she just means the last day in court? Faina must be an important lady for Zianne to invite her over. She's always looking for ways to climb the social ladder. Or gain juicy gossip.

"Thank you, Zianne. Your home is just stunning! You've been holding out on us."

Still listening intently, I turn back to the cheese pieces I've been wrapping in smoked salmon for an entrée.

"Move along, Fay!" a deep voice rumbles, sending goosebumps running across my skin. The male fae's voice seems to carry a warning in it. A hint of a temper and easy violence.

"Now, now, Armis. You won't miss out."

I don't catch his reply, but I'm not at all surprised by Zianne. If there is one thing I could admire about my stepmother, it is that she never allows herself to be cowered. Even if this man is a friend of hers, I'm sure he would still be intimidating to her.

"Good evening, Armis, Faina," Oriane's voice drifts through the house.

Three more fae arrive within the next ten minutes, and I hear them all move into the second sitting room, where their voices fade into an indistinguishable buzz. I have half an hour to have everything ready.

Once the salmon-cheese bites are finished, I slip into the dining room and set seven places for Zianne and her guests. I can't see them from here, as the second sitting room is on the other side of the house. The forks tinkle gently as I place them on the table.

I startle as laughter erupts from the sitting room, but I smile. Happy guests are a good sign. Tonight should go smoothly.

I run a hand down my apron, smoothing out the crinkles. I'm wearing the brown dress as Zianne ordered, but what will her guests say when they see my manacle? Maybe I should have checked if she really meant this one.

I shove the thought away. My stepmother knows what she's doing.

A soft breeze caresses my face, carrying Zianne's voice with it. "Shall we move into the dining room? My human should have everything ready by now."

The phrasing again strikes me as odd, but I hurry back into the kitchen to make sure the last touches for the meals are done.

"Is this starlight, Z?"

"You know it is, Fay," Zianne says lightly as I hear the chairs scrape at the table. "It belonged to my mother. She had the table specially made."

Their mindless chatter continues while I scoop up a jug of Zianne's finest iced tea, turn my eyes down, and enter the sitting room.

"This is your other *daughter*, then?" Armis grunts, his voice like sandpaper. I can see his bulky frame from the corner of my eye. Many of the fae are tall and lean, yet very strong. This man's strength is obvious for all to see.

"Yes," Zianne says carelessly. "Drop your suspicions, you old grouch. The girl won't talk."

"A lovely creature though, isn't she?" says a soft, male voice. But my skin crawls just as it did when Armis spoke.

"Yes, I particularly like her jewellery," Faina giggles.

My cheeks redden but I keep my eyes firmly down, yet away from my ankle, as I reach the table and begin to pour the tea into their pitchers. Zianne's orders ring in my ears. Tonight must go smoothly.

"It's taken so long for us to meet in person. We should try to do it more often," Faina says, and I feel everyone's attention leave me. Except the man who commented on my looks. I'm sure it's his gaze that I can feel studying me from head to toe.

I supress a shudder. But a soft laugh from Oriane pulls his interest away.

Every cup full without incident, I disappear back into the kitchen and re-emerge with the salmon entrée. As before, I start at the head of the table with Zianne and work my way around. She doesn't acknowledge me, doesn't move to make it easier for me to serve her food.

But she's busy speaking with her guests, so I shift carefully around her. Dodging her hands as they move enthusiastically.

Oriane is next. Her journal sits on the table beside her, cracked open to reveal a double-page spread of writing.

Then Faina. I don't dare look her in the eye, but the woman is unnaturally ... normal-looking for a fae. She doesn't carry the usually stunning beauty of her race, though she still outshines any human. Her hair is dark brown and short, not even reaching her shoulders.

She wears a leather outfit, at odds with the elegant dresses fae women normally choose to don. But even Oriane has shunned her normal revealing dresses for a silken tunic and pants tonight.

Somehow, I don't think this dinner is about their social status.

I place the tray down in the centre of the table and step back, head down and hands clasped behind my back. I let their words wash over me as my thoughts drift to the upcoming festival. And my dress. If the dinner ends early enough, I might be able to finish it tonight.

"GIRL!"

I jump a full foot in the air and run forwards. I can feel Armis's glower as I stop beside him.

"Deaf as well as dumb?" he growls. "I'll have more of the salmon."

My hands are shaking as I reach out to serve him. How long had he been trying to get my attention? *And why couldn't he serve himself?* my mind adds rebelliously.

"I'll have another one, too," the soft-spoken man says. I supress another shiver as I round the table. But as I lower the salmon and cheese bite to his plate, my eyes slip up to his face and I find his eyes already on me. And his face darkens.

"Filth!" he whispers. What happens next is over in the blink of an eye. One moment his hand is by his plate, the next it is arcing through the air, electricity dancing between his fingers, and slamming into my chest.

I cry out as the charge tears through my body and my hands seize, sending pieces of salmon off the tray and straight onto the shoulder of the man next to him. Even as the magic is still coursing through my veins, the other man jumps to his feet with a furious roar and slams his knuckles into my cheek.

And then I'm on the floor, every muscle in my body aching, my cheek pounding, and food strewn across the stones.

"Get up!" My stepmother's voice breaks the silence that had settled over the table. And Faina bursts into uproarious laughter. Oriane joins her.

"Oh, I don't know. Perhaps we should let the prince have his way at the festival. If this is what it will be like with the humans there!" Faina gasps through her giggles.

"Don't be a fool," Armis's deep voice rumbles, but he fails to hide his humour at the situation. "The brat needs to be taught a lesson just like this one. The humans will outnumber us soon. Something needs to change."

I pull myself onto my knees, my eyes watering, and quickly gather the splattered food from the floor, snatching up the tray. Biting my lip to keep the tears at bay, I limp into the kitchen.

Their voices trail after me.

"On that we can all agree," Zianne says. "But this new ambassador is going to make things difficult."

"Hardly, Mother," Oriane says. "Jorai just needs to be shown where his loyalties should lie. I'm sure he'll fall into line quickly enough."

"With a woman like you by his side, he certainly will." The man's voice is still calm, betraying nothing of what he just did to me. As though he hadn't just used his magic on me for simply looking him in the eye.

Who is this man? Whilst shifter magic is normal for any fae, any other form of magic, including elemental, is rare. It's usually only seen among the court or royals, at least in Ashennor. Which is why Zianne and Oriane are highly regarded. They have no special blood, and yet they possess rare magic.

This man could be anyone in the king's court.

"Thank you, Midian."

My face gives a hard throb. I can't afford to be standing here listening to them. I have a meal to serve and a debt to pay off. Closing my eyes, I take two deep breaths into my aching lungs to gather myself, scoop up the first part of their meal, and force myself back out.

"If he's insisting on inviting the scum, we will just have to discourage him." Oriane's face is lit up in a way I've never seen before, a disturbing gleam in her eyes.

The table is growing louder, the fae slamming their hands down, nodding fiercely. My heart is thundering in my chest, but I can't spare a thought for whatever it is they're planning involving Jorai. I just want to get through this dinner and go to bed and rest my aching body.

I don't look at anyone, not even Zianne. I just dodge fists, some aimed at me, some merely errant movements of impassioned speech. Globs of spit land on me as I duck and weave around the table, and I catch an elbow to my stomach, then retreat to the kitchen to prepare the next course. Their words flow over me unheard.

There is nothing but getting through this night and I move through it in a trance, forcing my mind to focus on the dress waiting for me in my room, and not on the beautiful but terrible fae plotting at the dinner table.

I finally fall into bed exhausted, covered in spit and food, every part of my body sore. My eyes well up again, and I curl in on myself, pulling my thin blanket close.

The night is a blur, but there's one thing that sticks out to me. None of them want any humans to attend the festival.

Not even Zianne and Oriane said anything to disagree. I was invited, my name was down, but what if I can't go? What if this dinner was just a sign of things to come?

A longing for my mother's arms like I haven't felt in years seizes me, and I find myself whisper-singing her favourite song. Sometime in the night my voice gives way to hers, singing through the dark recesses of my consciousness.

11

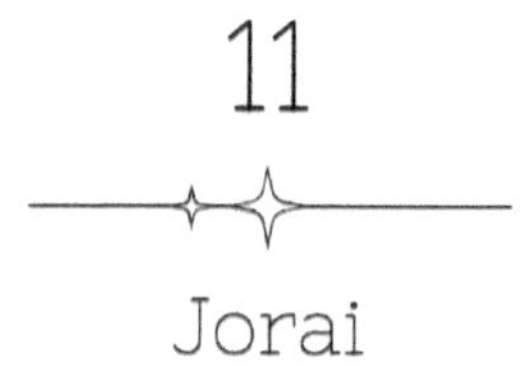

Jorai

RAIDEN'S EYES SCAN EVERY stall, item, and face that we pass in the markets. But there is nothing to see, just as I told him. Humans and fae mingle, moving freely among the stalls. Sure, many stay with their families or friends, but that's normal.

There's no hostility. No slaves. Everyone is happy. I can't stop the grin from spreading across my face.

"So, what food are we trying first, Your Highness?" he says, still taking everything in.

"Please, call me Jorai while you're here." I look around, trying to spot my favourite stall. It's been a while since I came down here, and my mouth waters at the thought.

Zephi taps my shoulder. "Over there, Your Highness."

Raiden laughs. "It must be good."

"Apparently, I am very predictable," I say ruefully.

We weave through the sea of people and shifted fae, but most of them move aside for our small entourage. I somehow managed to convince Zephi to bring just one other guard with us, so we don't make too big of a disturbance as we move about.

Still, Zephi has to turn away several rather excited-looking young women before we reach the stall. The smell is simply divine.

"Have you had these before?" I ask as I hand over a couple of coins.

"No," Raiden admits, "but I've seen children with them."

"See? I'm not the only one." Zephi nudges me in the ribs.

"Ah, but you were converted too." I turn to Raiden and wink. "You'll see."

My friend grins, taking one of the potato sticks for himself as I hand one to Raiden. It is a common food among the children, that's true. But there's a reason for it.

It's a sliver of potato, cut and woven around a stick, and fried in a herb-filled oil. And this stall cooks them until they're soft on the inside, but crunchy on the outside. A child's treat, but one I can never turn down.

We turn away with our food and continue through the aisles of stalls. Raiden bites into the potato and makes a sound of appreciation. Grinning, I go to take a bite of my own, but there's a commotion at the head of the aisle we're currently walking down. People are gathering by the wall of a building.

I exchange a questioning look with Zephi. Sometimes musicians come out to play or sing, but there's no hint of a tune in the air. And the voices of the crowd are growing louder. They're restless.

Food forgotten, I turn to Raiden. The disturbance hasn't gone unnoticed by him either. Raiden's hand rests on the hilt of a dagger strapped to his hip—his swords left in the palace today—relaxed but ready.

"I apologise, Ambassador," I use the word purposefully, trying to remind him of his reason for being here. That he is not a guard or warrior, but a politician. "But I think we'd better check this out."

"Of course," he says, his blue eyes locked on the growing crowd.

But I can hardly tell him to stay here, to not see whatever is happening down there. Not when to leave him alone could prove politically disastrous, even if he can look after himself. But the urge is inexplicably strong. I can't explain why.

We push through the crowd, Zephi moving to the front, his companion behind us. Other fae are following, drawn by the commotion, but others are leaving ... no, *humans* are leaving. Pushing through the crowd, casting *fearful* glances behind them.

My stomach drops. No. Not this. Not now.

"Make way," Zephi calls, as the throng grows thicker. "Make way."

And as the fae part, I can finally see what's caught their attention. The rebels have left their mark.

It's a strange sign, but its meaning is clear. Painted in red is one curved line, like the top of a human ear, and above it is the pointed line of a fae ear. Humans below fae. It's more common than I'd like to admit.

My eyes close. This is just the thing I didn't want Raiden to worry about. The rebels may be more active with the festival coming up, but it's just a scream to be noticed.

Snapping my eyes open, I turn back to the crowd. The buzz of voices slowly lowers to a mere whisper.

"Everyone is to return to their business. There is nothing to see here. The king remains firm on his stance against the rebels. Their voices will not be heard. Their opinions will not be affirmed. They represent what is no longer supported or upheld in our kingdom. The tantrum of a few spoiled children does not hold sway over our great people. These are nothing but empty threats."

But as everyone begins to turn away, I can still feel Raiden's eyes burning into the back of my head. The damage has been done.

·)⟩⟩●⟨⟨(·

The night after the fiasco at the markets sees me entertaining guests at the palace. It's a little pre-festival celebration for some of the members of court.

The gardens outside have been turned into something from a child's fairytale. Delicate fires, burning starlight to turn them silver, are dotted throughout, casting the fae in flickering silver light. The stars are bright this evening, though they will be brighter still for the festival, and provide their own white luminance. Though I can't see where it is coming from, the gentle music of several stringed instruments trickles over the crowd.

Weaving my way among the guests, I nod greetings to my father's friends, our extended family, and other court members. Every one of them has tried, or will try, to have my ear tonight. Though it's not unusual, there seems to be a certain ... fervour among the women.

"Your Highness," a young woman says, blocking my path to Aunt Cyra and Raiden, curtsying low. The move throws me an eyeful of her chest as I look down at her and I find myself quickly looking vaguely over her head.

"Oriane." I offer her my hand, gently pulling her up to a safe eye-line. "You look stunning."

Cyra would never let me move away from a single one of these women without offering a compliment. Most of this is for me, after all, though it feels vain to acknowledge. But they deserve my thanks.

"You're too kind, Prince Jorai. But it's just a little something my maid threw together." She smiles shyly, running a hand down the all-too-revealing blue dress.

Cyra glances over her shoulder at us, her eyes lingering on Oriane and her dress, but Raiden says something that draws her attention away.

"I hope it's not too early for me to wish you a happy birthday. I—" Oriane hesitates, her cheeks reddening "I have a present for you."

"Thank y—"

She leans in, much closer than royal protocol dictates, her sweet perfume surrounding me, and presses a soft kiss to my cheek. Without another word, she turns and hurries away.

"You certainly have a way with the ladies."

I slap the back of my hand against Zephi's chest as he stops beside me. I knew the captain would be somewhere among the crowd, though not as a guest tonight. His black and silver dress uniform doubles to serve as advertisement of the presence of my guards.

It's just my luck that Zephi would find me right in time for Oriane's 'gift'.

I wipe the cuff of my jacket against my cheek, hoping I'm not just smudging her lipstick further and turn to face him. "They're getting bolder."

"Oriane's always been open in her interest," Zephi says, his voice turning thoughtful. "Though, now I suppose they'll all be coming to offer ... *gifts*."

This time, I lightly punch his arm. "I really think you should shift tonight. You'll have less reason to get distracted from your duty as a wolf."

With a low chuckle, he disappears back into the crowd. Perhaps I should consider spending the rest of the night in my shifted form, as well. Many of the fae tend to avoid the large cat that I become. With a sigh, I continue on my way to my aunt. My father would never let me stay as the cat tonight.

"... I understand. I've been looking for my goddaughter and her father for some time, but with no luck. I wouldn't even know where to begin. Maaz could have taken her anywhere," Cyra says. Her eyes seem to be sparkling with a thin layer of water.

Cyra has a goddaughter? But I don't recognise the name of the fae male, Maaz. She's never mentioned him before. My brow furrows at this new information.

Raiden's face is grave. "The first step is the hardest. It took me weeks to find any sign of Zara, but it turned cold too quickly. If Maaz doesn't want to be found, it could be even harder to find them." He's wearing a white tunic with light blue hems, his swords across his back again. He looks the part of a warrior, but his voice is soft as he speaks to my aunt.

Cyra dabs at her eyes as I stop beside them. I turn to her, a question on the tip of my tongue, when Raiden speaks first.

"Prince Jorai, I'm surprised you managed to steal a moment from your guests."

"They seem to be particularly demanding tonight," I chuckle.

"Yes." Raiden's blue eyes lock with mine. "Can I have a word?"

I resist the urge to swallow heavily, to shift in place, and merely nod. I knew this was coming. And the fact that his walls are back up only confirms it. His easy smile and humour have been missing all day.

We step away from Cyra, into the shadow of a large tree. It's the most privacy we'll manage out here. While fae hearing is good, there is enough chatter to hopefully mask our words.

"I know what you're going to say," I cut Raiden off, unwilling to hear it. "But you don't need to worry about the rebels."

Raiden frowns. "I wouldn't be so quick to dismiss them," he says, slowly. "Even a minority can cause trouble. And I doubt they are so few in number as you hope."

I shake my head.

"It's no secret your father was reluctant entering into our alliance. Your people reflect his views."

"My father is a good man," I hiss. "There is nothing to worry about." I feel as though I'm stuck repeating the same thing over and over. "You saw the people mingling at the markets yesterday, and you'll see it again at the festival."

Raiden's expression is all too knowing. "Even a great leader can fail to see what's wrong with his people."

My jaw clenches. "I assure you, there is no mistreatment of humans happening here. I would know."

He tilts his head, sending silver firelight flickering across his face as his eyes close off, but Raiden merely nods. "Excuse me, I did not mean to offend."

And just like that, he's gone.

Sighing heavily through my nose, I turn back towards my guests searching for the drink table. But Raiden's words echo in my mind. And I can't help but notice the lack of a single curved ear in the gardens.

"Jorai!"

"Not now," I murmur, tugging at the collar of my jacket. Why did I wear this tonight? It's too warm.

"Jorai!"

I plaster a smile on my face and turn around. "Father."

"Was that young Oriane I saw offering her well wishes?" He winks, taking a sip from a glass. The smell of wine hits me as he leans in, the liquid splashing up and leaving a drop on his sleeve. "She's a beauty."

I grimace, all too aware that the ambassador is still somewhere in the gardens, likely watching our every move.

"Father," I say, reaching for his glass, but he tugs it away with a frown. "Ambassador Raiden might wish to speak with you tonight."

"Why?" His frown deepens. "Is something wrong? You're meant to be handling this, Jorai."

"I am." The words come out harsher than I mean them to, but what is he thinking getting tipsy on a night like this? "But *you* are the king."

"That I am. And I'll speak to him when *I'm* ready." He looks around, his blue eyes lingering on the young court ladies. "I trust you've been entertaining these young women? Any one of them would—"

"I know," I grind out.

"Unless your desires have already settled?" he says, his tone hardening in warning. I follow his gaze to Oriane, who throws back her head and laughs at something Midian, a member of our court with control over electricity, has said.

I feel nothing at the sight of them talking. In fact, I hope he steals Oriane's attentions away from me. There's no spark between us, and I don't want there to be.

"No. Not yet."

He slaps a hand to my back rather forcefully. "Then get back out there."

12

Kaylin

I JOLT UPRIGHT AT the sound of Oriane and Zianne arriving home, glancing around the dark workroom in sleep-addled confusion. I've fallen asleep over my dress at the table, and the low-burning candles reveal that its grown very late. They must have had a good night.

I'm just twisting to get up when I hear Zianne's voice from behind me.

"What's this?"

I freeze at her tone.

"It's my dress for tomorrow." The words send a throb through my bruised cheek.

"For tomorrow? Whatever do you mean, Kaylin?" Her eyes are like thunder. Oriane stands behind her, her face alight with joy.

"You said—"

"—that you would only be coming if you behaved well, and all your chores were done."

"Yes, and I have. All my jobs are finished."

"But look at this room!"

My heart sinks even as I frown in confusion. I look around. The workroom is the cleanest it's been since before the invitations were sent out. "What about it?"

"Why, it's a pigsty!"

A rush of wind barrels through the room, tearing fabric from the shelves, sending buttons shooting into the air, and a pile of pins scattering.

"It's disgusting, Kaylin!" Zianne says, her eyes now positively gleaming as she finally steps inside the room. She tugs my dress out from under my hand, holding it up. "You can't honestly expect to go wearing this?"

Oriane hurries over, snatching the dress I've worked on in every spare moment from her mother's hands. "And with this massive tear down the front?"

"No!" I shout, but it's too late. With a loud ripping sound, the seams give out, and the bust folds in.

Zianne's hand seems to appear out of thin air, slamming into my face, right on my bruised cheek. The move knocks me straight out of my chair.

"And then there's your attitude, Kaylin!" She's roaring now, her magic trembling through the room as her emotions run out of control.

I cower below her, my arms over my head.

"Did you really think I would ignore your behaviour towards my guests? That I would turn a blind eye and let you go to the festival when you can't even show respect to my friends?" she seethes.

"Or maybe," Oriane whispers, but the words seem loud enough to make me flinch, likely pushed by her own magic, "she thought the prince would actually be interested in her."

The wind stops.

"Is that true? You think Prince Jorai would be interested in a human slave?"

My eyes widen. I don't know what's happening here, but I've never heard the tone in Zianne's voice before. I sink further down to the floor, pressing my face to the stone at her feet.

"No, never! I just—I just wanted to see the palace. That's all."

The minutes trickle by in silence. I can almost hear the thoughts whirling around her mind. I practically grew up in the palace while my mother worked there. It could be a genuine desire of mine. And indeed, it is, though I had wished to at least glimpse Jorai.

"Well, you won't be going, will you? Not with this mess to clean up. You have a debt to pay off, Kaylin," Stepmother sneers.

I watch Zianne's bare feet turn away, then Oriane's as she follows her mother, but I stay pressed into the stone for another five minutes. I can hear them talking quietly in the sitting room, even as tears trickle down my face.

"Kaylin." Zianne's voice is gentle as she calls from the other room, as though she hadn't just been in here raging at me. "It's time for bed. You've got a big day tomorrow. Get downstairs for some rest."

"Ye—" I clear my throat. "Yes, Stepmother."

·)➤●⳺(·

It feels as though time has slowed down to a barely imperceptible pace as I get started on the workroom. But even once I finish in here, Zianne has sourced more jobs for me to do to keep me busy while they're gone.

It takes two hours to pack away all the fabric the way I'd had it; by colour and material. The buttons and pins take even longer, and I'm pulled away to serve Zianne and Oriane a light lunch before helping them dress. The festivities start at dusk, but they both want to look stunning.

Zianne is first. I braid her long, silken hair into a crown atop her head and weave a string of starlight gems through it before pulling a curl of hair loose on either side of her face to fall in front of her ears. Her makeup is heavy, with golden eyeshadow and a red lipstick that stands out against the black dress that drapes across her body, falling dangerously low over her back.

Oriane is unable to hide her excitement as I dust silver over her eyelids.

"I can't wait to see Jorai's face when he sees me," she says, staring over my shoulder at her reflection in the mirror.

"He thought I looked so beautiful last night, and when we kissed, I just knew he was the one."

I barely stop my hand from jolting and spreading silver across her cheek. Her eyes flicker to mine, and her grin doesn't quite meet her eyes as I slide her mask into place.

"If he only kissed me after last night, I wonder what he'll do after seeing me in this."

My blood runs cold, then hot. I swallow heavily. "Let's get you into your dress, then."

"I want the house spotless when we return," Zianne says as Oriane steps into the back of the carriage they've hired for the night. "You're not to come to the festival."

She injects a little bit of magic into her words, simply willing that they be binding and true, but there's no need. I have nothing to wear, no way to get there even if I did, and the cleaning still has to be done. Her magic might wear off in an hour or two, but it may as well hold me all night.

The carriage pulls away as soon as Zianne is inside. There is no door to enclose them within, so I can see the glee on their faces as they disappear down the road.

Closing my eyes, I allow myself just a moment to imagine I were with them, my own dress spilling over the edge of the seat, tickling my legs. My hair would have been up, braids holding it in place.

I let the image run until I arrive at the palace, for I assume it's happening there, and Jorai's eyes lock with mine as I step down from the carriage. And recognition lights in his eyes.

Sighing, I open my eyes and turn around to look over the house.

"There's no use moping; there's work to be done," I whisper.

Trudging inside to fetch a rope basket, I make my way back outside to the line spread between two large oak trees in the back garden. I washed clothes for Zianne and Oriane this morning, and they were probably dry hours ago with this heat, but I didn't have the chance to bring them in with all the work preparing for the festival.

I run my fingers across the dress Oriane wore last night, the one that Jorai kissed her in. My heart gives a painful throb at the thought.

Perhaps he doesn't know what she's really like? Or has my friend really changed so much in the years since I saw him last? For a moment, I'm lost in memories of him. Of running around the palace, reading books together, and copying my mother and his aunt while they had tea.

I pause, my thoughts sidetracked. I never did find out how their friendship began, but it brought my mother so much joy. My chest gives another throb.

A bird is calling in the distance, a gentle clicking, curious sound, but I'm too lost in my thoughts to notice it much. My hands keep working, my mind far away. Until the bird lets out one long cry and something deep inside me stirs at the familiar sound.

My head snaps up and, squinting against the sun, I spot her, as though summoned by my thoughts.

A beautiful white swan crests the roof of the house, and her long neck twists as though she is searching for something. It's been years since I last saw a swan, and that one wasn't a true swan. But this bird, her feathers so smooth she gleams in the afternoon sun, isn't her. It couldn't be.

But her black eyes land on me, and a heartbreaking sound of pure joy cracks through the air.

"No," I gasp, hands flying to my mouth. My cheeks are wet; tears have spilled unbidden down my face.

The swan swoops down, landing gracefully in the grass in front of me, calling incessantly even as she stands up, her wings flapping. Her body begins to elongate, her feathers retract, her beak shrinks, and arms and legs begin to form, curly blonde hair sprouting from her head, and her eyes lighten from black to bright green.

"Cyra!" I throw myself into my godmother's arms, Jorai's aunt.

"Kaylin! Oh! I've been looking for you everywhere. But I didn't know where you two could have gone!" she gushes, her arms tight around me. "I heard your father had left Zianne's employ, but then Oriane mentioned her maid had made her beautiful dress! And I knew it had to be you."

"My father did leave." My voice is muffled against her shoulder, though I'm bending slightly to hug her. I never realised just how short she was for a fae. I subtly tug at the skirt of my dress, making sure it's sitting low around my feet. "I've taken his place."

"But I came looking for you." Cyra pulls back, frowning, tears shining in her eyes. "I came after your mother died, and Zianne said you two were gone. But she didn't know where you were headed!"

My heart aches, and I can't hold her eyes. I know the very day she's speaking of; it was the day I truly understood my place.

Zianne used her blood magic to keep me quiet in my bedroom while she entertained Cyra upstairs. My stepmother didn't want any trouble when I still had so much work to do. Cyra was so close, but she'd never been so far. I never tried to reach her after that.

"I—I came back." I stutter around the lie, but it's easier than the truth.

"But what about your father?"

"He couldn't stand it here anymore." I swallow thickly. Another lie. He'll be back once I've paid off his debt. Some days it's harder to believe than others, but he'll be back.

"Maaz could never stay away from you for long," Cyra says, echoing my thoughts. Her frown slowly clears, and a smile takes its place again. "Well, never mind! Let me look at you!"

She pulls further back, her eyes travelling over me once, then twice. I shift in place, suddenly very aware of the dirt on my clothes, my messy hair, and the bruise on my face.

"You're beautiful!" Tears stream from her eyes. "But what happened here?" She gently places her hand against my cheek, and I can't help but close my eyes against her gentle touch. It's something I haven't felt in years.

"Nothing," I say through a thick throat. I don't want to tell her about Zianne's friends, not after the way my stepmother raged yesterday. I still have years here, and I can't afford to offend her again, to rock this barely balancing boat. "I tripped while cleaning."

"But why aren't you at Jory's birthday? He'd be so excited to see you!"

"I—I don't have a dress, and I have so much to do! Zianne has lots of jobs for me to get done before she gets home."

"Oh." Cyra waves a hand. "I can deal with all that. I can even hide this nasty bruise."

My mouth drops open. I can't go to the festival. If Zianne saw me there—if she got back before me ...

I voice my doubts.

"I can deal with that too." She winks, gently wiping the tears from my cheeks. "Let me do this for you, darling. And then we have so much catching up to do."

"I—" Just one night. One night of happiness. One night of something for myself.

And then I'll return to paying off my father's debts without complaint. Just one night.

"Yes! Let's do it." I hesitate. There are just a couple of problems, one of which Cyra can't know about. "But I need a long dress that goes past my ankles, and are you sure Zianne won't recognise me? I don't want to get in trouble."

"Done, and don't worry, I'm positive."

13

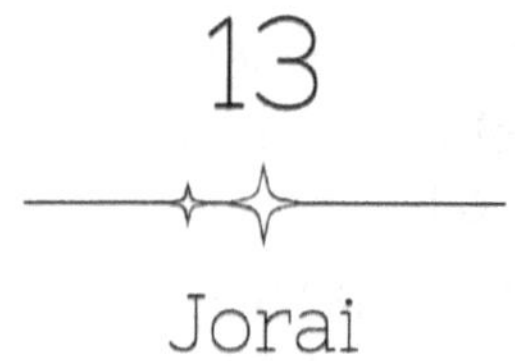

Jorai

THE FIRST NIGHT OF the festival officially starts at dusk, but guests begin arriving over an hour early. The starlight—intricate swirls and vines—in my black tunic shines as I pass the silver bonfire already burning fiercely at the centre of the hill.

The palace gleams below us in the distance, the city spread around it. Behind me is the beginning of the Ereas Forest, and to the right is the road leading back down to the city, already crowded with fae and humans arriving on foot, by horse, or by carriage. One or two even arrive in their animal forms, unusual for formal events but not unheard of.

Zephi and a handful of guards greet them all as they arrive, their gazes darting over each and every guest. It should be enough to put the rebels on edge.

Music sweeps over me, light and airy. Happy. A mixture of strings and flutes, the musicians stand off to the side near the refreshments. Fae and humans are already dancing by the fire, hiking up their dresses or shedding their jackets as they take to the grass around the bonfire.

The festivities have begun.

It seems as though every fae woman—and even several human women—in all of Ashennor comes to greet me and wish me well for my birthday.

And I'm forced to engage with each one of them, offering them a charming conversation that I know they will repeat every word of to their friends and families.

But my father's eyes are on me; though I haven't spotted him yet, I can feel him.

Raiden arrives as the sky begins to darken, escorted by Taavi and another of Zephi's guards, and I offer him a nod of greeting. He returns it, and I'm surprised to find the gesture isn't at all stiff. I only saw him very briefly at breakfast this morning, an impossibly short time to judge his mood after yesterday.

I grin. He's giving me a chance to prove it all to him. And a chance to save this friendship with Frigarth. I won't waste it.

"Jorai!"

A young lady appears in front of me, and my eyes widen. "Oriane."

Her dress is ... *revealing*. Silver in colour, the top layer is not only see-through, but it plunges in a sharp V nearly all the way to her navel. Underneath is a simple, very small covering to hide her underwear.

I don't know where to turn my eyes and finally settle with locking them onto her grey ones shining from under a layer of silver glitter. Her mask is nothing more than a silver wire frame over her eyes with lace strung between the gaps. Starlight practically covers her very being.

She smiles. "I haven't been able to stop thinking about last night."

I frown.

She blushes. "I'm not sorry I was so forward, but I am sorry if I embarrassed you."

"Oh!" *Oh.* "The kiss. Right. Don't worry about it."

Her smiles widens. *Wait.*

"I mean—"

"I hope you'll pardon my forwardness again in that case. Will you dance with me tonight?"

My eyes trail past her head as I try to work a way out of this. I can hardly turn Oriane down. But everything about her feels fake and forced, like she's trying just a little too hard.

And in the dress she's wearing, I'm afraid she'll have a wardrobe malfunction if we were to dance together—I feel my lips part.

"Jorai? What?" Vaguely I'm aware of Oriane turning to follow my distracted gaze.

She's—she's beautiful. Whoever she is. But only a princess could afford to look that stunning.

Her dress is a russet red-brown, layered like Oriane's with a lighter, see-through fabric. The skirt goes down to her feet, bare like mine and many of the other fae.

If my aunt were here, she would be fawning over the entire thing. The sleeves hang low off her shoulders, but a twisting vine clearly shaped from starlight seems to rise from the fabric over her chest, coming up over her shoulders like a strap. Silver flowers and vines decorate the V-neckline, spreading down her torso and disappearing into the skirt. I see it all in a second, because it's her face that holds my attention.

She seems to be positively shining. Not just from the delicate layer of makeup spread over her lips and cheeks, or the mask covering a large portion of her face, but from some kind of inner joy. A pure form of happiness. I haven't seen anyone this happy in a long time. It's magnetic.

"Jorai!" Oriane's voice calls from behind me, and somehow it seems I've left her behind, crossing through the crowd to the young woman being waved through by Zephi.

Her brown eyes find mine just as I'm barely a step away from her, and they widen in surprise. I might have a mask on, but it's not hard to tell who I am with the crown my father insisted I wear tonight.

I stop before her. "Hello."

14

Kaylin

C YRA GETS OUT OF the carriage before we even crest the hill. "I'll be right behind you, love. We'd just better avoid Zianne seeing us together."

A nervous nod is all I can manage. Maybe this was a terrible idea. If anyone recognises me ... I shudder at the thought of my stepmother's rage.

My godmother, now in a pale green dress lined with emeralds, squeezes my hand and turns to leave.

"Wait!" she says, spinning back around. Cyra flicks her fingers, then begins to twirl her hand. A small flower forms in her hand. Red and delicate, with only four petals, she tucks it into my hair. "To match the dress."

Her hand lingers on my face, then she winks and disappears.

I run a hand down my dress. It's one of Cyra's, made specially for the festival, and I had to drop the hem, but you can hardly tell unless you know what to look for. I can't believe I'm wearing this. I can't believe I'm here.

The festival was meant to start at dusk, yet it becomes all too clear as the driver halts at the end of the road that most of the guests arrived early. But none of that matters as my eyes sweep over the hillside.

Fae and human alike have already begun to dance by the massive silver bonfire, their bodies jumping and swaying in time with the lively tune fae musicians are playing from beside an oaken table of refreshments. Vines are woven up the table's legs, spreading out between the platters of food and pitchers of drink.

"Miss?"

I jolt. The carriage driver, Geralt, stands beside me, hand out to help me down.

Cyra said he was a servant from the palace. He looks to be around the age my father would be, with grey hair and kind green eyes. I felt myself warming to him the instant we met at Zianne's estate.

He didn't ask any questions, even though he'd arrived with a handful of other servants who had come to clean the house.

"Thank you." I take his hand in one of my own and carefully hold the hem of my dress low enough to hide my ankles, but high enough not to trip as I climb down. It's a delicate art.

"Will you be attending tonight?" I ask the man, pressing at the mask on my face. It hasn't moved an inch, but I can't help worrying about it slipping.

He tugs at his tunic, a twinkle lighting in his eye. "I will be there. Lady Cyra asked that I get you home before Zianne and her daughter?"

"Yes, please."

"I'll fetch you when it's time."

"Thank you so much, Geralt."

As he climbs back into the carriage to find somewhere to park, I turn back to the hillside and feel a grin spreading across my face.

I'm moving forwards without even realising, my eyes drinking up every inch of the party.

The leafy archway spun with flowers and vines that acts as an entryway, the dresses and tunics, the otherworldly flickering flames that must be costing the palace a fortune alone to run, and the fae. They're normally stunning, normally beyond anything a human could ever hope to be, but tonight, tonight they are a dream.

Movement in front of me draws my eyes, and it takes all my strength not to gasp and scream and shout.

Because it's Jory. There's no mistaking those ice-blue eyes. The brown hair, shorter than I remember, and that smile. That smile pierces right through to my heart.

But the rest is unfamiliar. He's no longer the little boy I played with.

He has to be nearly a foot taller than me, with broad shoulders and a strong jawline. A black jacket lined with starlight sits over a grey tunic and black pants. His feet, like most fae, are bare. A silver band lies on his head, carved with oak leaves and apple blossoms.

Strength and peace. An apt image of the prince I remember.

"Hello."

It takes me longer than I'd like to admit to be able to form a response, and when I do, it comes out as a squeak. "Hi."

A grin tugs at his mouth, and I just about lose the air in my lungs at the rush of homesickness in my stomach as his eyes slide over me again.

"You are the most beautiful fae here."

I swallow thickly, resisting the urge to run a finger over the jewelled cuff under my hair that gives the illusion of pointed ears. Just another layer to my disguise should my hair happen to move and someone get a glimpse of my ears.

Don't correct him. Don't tell him. He can't know what you are now.

"Th—thank you."

Jorai doesn't notice the falter of my smile before I manage to muster it back. But I don't care. This is more than I ever hoped for. More than I ever dreamed.

To actually speak with him. To see for myself that he's OK.

He looks more than healthy, if the muscles rippling under his jacket are anything to go by, and his eyes are shining.

"Would you like to dance with me?"

"Oh." I haven't danced, well, ever. Unless you count the time I gate-crashed Jory's lessons and we ended up spinning wildly around the room until we fell to the floor too dizzy to stand. I wonder if he remembers that. "I don't really know how."

"I'm sure we can work something out." He holds out his hand, and before I can tell myself it's a mistake, I've placed my own hand in his and he's leading me towards the bonfire.

Someone bumps into me, and my heart drops as I turn to see Oriane.

"Oh, I'm so sorry," she says, her voice sickeningly false.

I can't speak to her. She might not recognise me, but my voice would be a giveaway. But before I can decide what to do, Jorai tugs on my hand, oblivious to the altercation, and I allow myself to be pulled along. It's a move so much like our childhood days running through the palace that my smile widens.

He stops as we reach the ring of fae and humans beside the fire and turns to me. His scent washes over me, and it's like we've never been parted. Earthy, like rain before a storm. Jorai's magic has always clung to him like that.

"Your hands go here," he explains, moving my hands into place, one in his own hand and one on his shoulder. "Mine goes here."

His hand slips into position at my waist. We only held hands that time we spun together.

"By the way," he says, looking down at me. "What's your name?"

I splutter. My name. I didn't even—I never thought—

"It's OK," he says after a long moment, his brow creasing. "I'll get it out of you later. I'm Jorai."

I'm so stunned at his declaration of finding out my name that I can't form any words for a full beat. There's no way I can tell him who I am. "It's nice to meet you, Your Highness."

"No," he says, as a drum joins the beat. "Just Jorai."

And then he sweeps me away. We swirl and skip, whirling around the other couples even as he releases me to spin under his arm. My feet catch on the hem of my dress, but I don't dare raise it out of my way.

Then I'm in his arms again and we're jumping and swaying, moving in one huge circle around the bonfire, its silver flames flickering off the lines of Jorai's jacket. The heat stings at my face, but I don't care. I give myself over to this moment.

We're gasping for breath when the song ends, but as I move to step away from him, Jorai's smile widens. "Another?" he asks eagerly.

I bite my lip, unable to hide my own smile. "Yes."

He shrugs out of his jacket, just as the Captain of the Royal Guard is passing. The fae male I saw in the markets with Zianne and Oriane. The man stops beside us.

"Jacket?" he says, his eyes twinkling as he takes it from Jorai.

"Thanks, Zeph."

"Just don't forget I'm a captain, not a maid."

I can't stop the small chuckle from slipping through my lips. As the captain's eyes land on me, I suck in a breath. Would this man recognise me?

But no recognition shines in his eyes as he looks down at me. I suppose if Oriane and Jorai can't see it's me, then neither would this man. But I can't forget the way he made sure I was invited despite Zianne's fake excuses.

"I don't believe we've met before, my lady. You look radiant tonight."

I clear my throat. "Thank you, Captain."

The next song has already started, and I can feel the glares from the partners around us. Our little group is right in the way.

"Right," Jorai says, his hands sliding back into place. "We have a dance to … dance." He winces.

But Zephi grins, nodding, and disappears, even as Jorai sweeps me away again.

By the third dance, the music just as lively and fast as before, my breaths are coming in deep gasps. I've never moved so much in my life, but I never want to stop. When the music ends, even Jorai is puffing.

"Let's get a drink," he suggests, leaning close so I can hear him.

He holds my hand as we push through the crowd together, our arms brushing with each step. But I don't move away. I couldn't even if I wanted to with the number of bodies on either side of us.

The oaken table we stop in front of is covered with glasses full of red, silver, and golden liquids, and even some with crystal clear water.

"Have you had loi before?" he asks me.

I hesitate. I've not tried the fermented drink before, though I did sneak one of the berries from storage once. "No," I finally say. I've not had anything fermented before, but I've heard it's a weak drink. Most fae have it for the taste more than anything else.

"Here," he says, scooping up two glasses of golden liquid and handing me one. My eyebrows rise. The berries themselves are a bright purple.

"It's fine," Jorai says, seeing my surprise. "The colours change depending on the process used to make it. This has been mixed with juice from kilan berries."

That explains the golden colour.

I take a tentative sip, the flavour bursting on my tongue. "This is amazing!"

Jory grins, sipping from his own even as I take a large gulp. An explosion bursts inside my mouth, sweet but with a slight tang, the drink seems to fizz as it goes down. It reminds me of a sweet I once had a child, but a thousand times better. Loi berries are known for their delicious taste, but this is something else.

"I'm glad you like it." His eyes haven't left me this entire time, and I feel my cheeks heating. I look away, and my eyes land on Cyra barely two meters away.

She stands beside a tall fae man, rippling with muscles. His hair is so light it's nearly white. Two swords are strapped across his back with some kind of dual scabbard. But his demeanour seems kind, if a little rough around the edges.

"I believe you promised me a dance, Ambassador," I hear her shout over the music.

He bows, grinning. "I believe I did, my lady."

"Why haven't I seen you before?"

Jorai's voice drags my eyes back to him, the drink catches in my throat, and I'm sent into a coughing fit.

"I'm not from around here," I lie.

"No," he says, gently pushing a strand of hair back from my face. I'm all too aware of his touch, but his hand drops away before it reaches my ear. "I would remember you."

My heart thuds loudly in my chest, and for a moment I wonder if Zianne's guest has returned to hit me with his electric magic. But a quick glance around reveals that Midian isn't anywhere near us. *He doesn't know you,* my mind whispers in response to my confusion. The ache inside grows. *He doesn't remember, Kaylin.*

"What is it?" he whispers, stepping so close I can smell him again.

"Nothing," I say, forcing a smile. "I'm sorry it took so long to see you."

It's not a lie.

"Me, too." His grin is back, brighter than ever before. "Come, I love this song."

And we're back by the bonfire in time to slip seamlessly back between the dancers. The drum has dropped away, and the strings are louder, slower. And a woman's voice floats through the air. I know this song, it's one my mother used to sing to me and my father. About a man searching for his lost love. He travels over mountains, valleys, oceans, to find her. I hum along.

Jorai's arms slip around my waist, and I find my arms at his shoulders. And we're moving, swaying together, his eyes on mine, and it's like a dream. A dream I never want to wake from.

We're not even a full minute into the dance, when there's a tap at my shoulder, and I jolt, turning to see Geralt.

"Your pardon, my lady," he says bowing his head. Cyra may have gone a little overboard with the instructions. "I'm afraid it's time to leave."

"Thank you, Geralt." I lower my arms from Jorai's shoulders, trying to ignore the stab in my chest. His hands stay at my waist.

"Leave? But it's barely midnight."

"I'm sorry," I say, forcing myself to take a step back as I look up into his oh-so-familiar eyes. His hands fall away. "I really must go."

I'm already starting to walk away, but he follows.

"Will I see you tomorrow?"

"I—I don't know."

Geralt's hand is at my back, urging me onwards.

"Please, say you'll be here tomorrow."

We're pushing through the crowd, the distance between us growing.

"I can't." I hope he can hear the reluctance, the pain in my voice. I wish I could promise him another night. Another hundred nights. But the dream is already ending.

His disappointed eyes are the last thing I see before the crowd swallows him up.

15

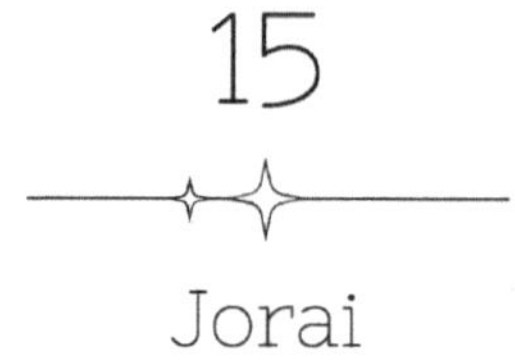

Jorai

Raiden leans back in his chair, a cup of hot coffee in his hands.

"Things went well last night," he says, a hint of approval in his voice.

I grin, looking at him over my breakfast even as an image of the girl from the festival flashes in my mind. "It did." I pause as what he said registers. He means his concerns about the humans. I knew it. I knew he'd come around.

"Tonight will be even better."

His brow rises. "I suspect we're no longer speaking about the same thing."

"I—"

"Everyone saw you with the girl, Your Highness." He winks.

"I've never met anyone like her ... I don't even know her name." I sigh. I hope she comes tonight. Last night was the best night I've had in a long time, and all we did was dance.

Raiden tilts his head. "She left early, though, didn't she?"

I frown. "She did."

Did I misread her? I think back over the night, at the way she seemed to glow with joy. No, I'm sure she felt that connection. The same one I did. Something must have called her away.

"Well, I'm sure she'll—"

A throat clears, announcing the presence of a messenger. He hurries into the room.

"Your Highness!"

Raiden and I both straighten, the lightness of our conversation gone. He's suddenly a foreign ambassador again, and I'm a prince. Why was I even talking about the girl with him?

"What is it?"

The messenger glances at Raiden, his frown showing his exact thoughts on the man. Then he hands me a small piece of parchment.

My heart jolts as I look down at the note scrawled in Zephi's small writing. The rebels. Again.

I can feel Raiden's eyes on me, and I raise my own to meet his gaze. I'm not about to keep this from him. Something tells me that the friendship of our nations depends on me trusting Raiden. On him seeing what we do.

"The rebels have issued another threat. It seems they didn't enjoy the festivities."

"What will you do?" His voice is careful, controlled.

"We need to meet with my father, Cyra, and the Captain of the Guards." I stand, the remnants of food long forgotten.

"We?" He raises a curious brow.

"Yes, Ambassador. I would like you to come."

He nods his acceptance, taking a last swig of his coffee as he stands. The grey tunic is the most relaxed I've ever seen his ensemble, though his weapons remain strapped to him. No doubt there are some I can't even see. But he still looks the part. Still looks a warrior.

I lead the way through the palace, Raiden silent beside me. My thoughts are swirling. Bouncing between the rebels, the festival, the girl.

The girl. I have to see her again. I shake my head; I need to concentrate on this meeting.

Zephi and my father are already waiting for us, sitting in silence in my father's office. The air is thick with tension, but Cyra bounces in moments after us. Nothing seems to dampen her spirits. And she seems particularly happy today.

"What was the message?" I direct my question at Zephi. I doubt my father could be bothered to read it all. He's shown very little interest in the rebels.

"The festival is no longer to go ahead, or they will be attending," Zephi says, his deep voice rough with anger.

"That's just silly," Cyra says, perching on the edge of a chair. "What can they do about it?"

Raiden remains silent. Though I've invited him in, it's not his place to advise us unless it concerns Frigarth. Or unless I ask him directly.

I nod, but my thoughts are back on the girl. They never really left.

"It doesn't change anything. We cannot afford to budge for them." I turn to Zephi. "We'll need more guards."

He nods, opening his mouth to speak.

But my father lets out a loud sigh.

I glance at him. "What is it, Father?"

"I will not be dictated to this way," he says, his voice dangerously low. "I want them found. I want them in chains."

I exchange a look with Zephi. It's not like we haven't tried to find them.

"Of course, Father." What else is there to say?

"Tell me about the girl," he grunts.

I raise my eyebrows. That's it? He's not at all concerned about the rebels? Isn't that why we're here?

"Ohh, do!" Cyra squeals, her eyes lighting up.

Oh, great. I should have known this was coming. I'm meant to be searching for a wife. But somehow, the idea doesn't seem so bad when I think of the girl whose name I don't even know. And though there are more important things we should be discussing, I acquiesce.

"Well? Who is she?" my father demands.

"I don't know." I shrug, trying to seem light-hearted. If I even see her again, my father could scare her off with his talk about marriage.

"You don't know who she is," he repeats, his face darkening.

"But I'm hoping to see her again tonight," I hurry to add. Unfortunately, *I* can't run away at the mention of marriage.

He nods, mollified. "Good."

Raiden and Zephi have remained silent throughout this entire discussion, but I feel their presence like a heavy blanket. This is not the conversation I needed Raiden to hear.

"And what about the rebels?" I prod, trying to direct him back to why we're all here.

"Empty threats, as usual." He waves a dismissive hand.

"We have to send a message to them," I insist. While I doubt they could ever do anything to cause us any real harm, it would be foolish to ignore their threats.

"Do what you want. Increase the guards. Screen the guests. Go ahead with the festival."

It's a blunt dismissal but we accept it, nodding shallow bows as we leave. Cyra hurries to walk with me, her curls bouncing.

"Tell me about the girl, Jorai," she says, smiling. "She looked beautiful! And that dress! I'm so jealous."

I can't help the smile that returns to my face. "She was stunning, wasn't she?"

Cyra half giggles, half squeals. "And what else? You danced for hours!"

I look down at her, shaking my head as I find her hanging on to my every word. "It doesn't matter. I don't even know who she is, and she didn't know if she was coming back." My eyes trail away from my aunt's. "I've never met anyone like her, Cyra. She didn't care who I was."

She never once looked at my crown. It was refreshing.

"She'll be back," Cyra promises, her tone suddenly serious. I frown, looking back at her. She grins. "Who could resist you?"

I hear Zephi snort from behind us and pointedly ignore him.

"You think?" I frown, realising how that sounded. "I meant—about her coming tonight."

Raiden laughs but takes pity on me. "The girl will be back, Jorai. She was just as mesmerized as you were."

I stumble to a stop and laugh. "You three!"

"I haven't said anything!" Zephi frowns, but I can see the ghost of the smile he's trying to hide.

"You didn't have to." I shake my head, but I'm glad for this. For them.

But I sigh as my thoughts turn back to the rebels. The lightness of this moment is gone in an instant. "Come on, we need to get more soldiers organised for tonight."

Every second of my morning seems to be taken up by running around after soldiers and the festival organisers. Zephi handles briefing the guards, organising what each of them will do, where each will stand or patrol through the night.

Raiden accompanies me as I seem to walk through the entire palace, then turn around and do it again. There's no reason for him to, but he does anyway. Even as I'm making sure the rebels won't be able to cause trouble tonight, my thoughts keep returning to the girl.

Where is she? Is she out in the city even now? Does she know the hold she seems to have over me?

"Taavi!" I call, catching a glimpse of the guard's long black hair as he turns a corner. He backtracks, reappearing. "I've been looking for you."

"What is it, Your Highness?"

"Did Zephi find you?" I inquire.

I personally requested Taavi's involvement tonight. Even if he won't fight me, he is a good warrior. And even better, he has magic. The man could be invaluable tonight.

He frowns, puzzled. "No."

"You're being called in to service tonight. We've had another threat frrom the rebels. Report to Captain Zephi for your orders."

His expression clears, and he pushes his shoulders back. "Right away, Your Highness."

Taavi bows, then hurries in the direction of Zephi's office. I watch him go. Surely, this will all be more than enough. The rebels couldn't possibly be big enough to take us on.

"There's only so much you can do, Your Highness," Raiden says, echoing my thoughts.

His blue eyes are locked on Taavi as well.

"Thank you, Raiden." *For not giving up on us yet.*

The ambassador seems to hear my unspoken words, and nods. But all he says is, "Your parties are better than ours."

"Well—" I clap his shoulder "—you've got two more days of it."

When lunch finally comes, my heart seems to speed up. I can get ready for the second night of festivities to begin. I'm that much closer to seeing her again.

I just hope Cyra and Raiden are right. That she'll be there.

Because if she is, it means that she *wants* to be there. That whatever made her leave last night isn't enough to keep her away.

"Are you ready, Your Highness?" Zephi's voice calls from behind the curtain to my room.

I tug at my tunic and fix the collar of my jacket. "Ready."

He pulls back the fabric, sticking his head through. "The king wants your approval of the new arrangements before it starts."

"Has he seen it?" I raise an inquisitive brow.

Zephi gives me a look that tells me everything. "Your father is still in his office."

"Right," I sigh. "Let's go."

16

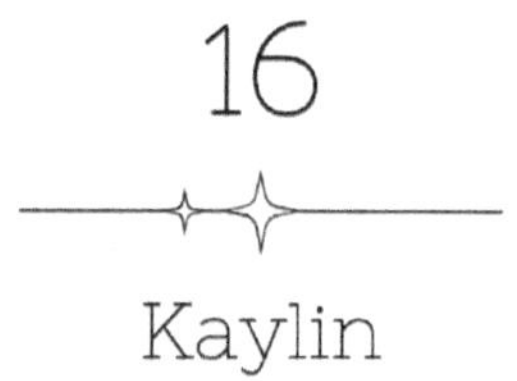

Kaylin

"Bᴜᴛ ᴡʜᴏ ᴡᴀs sʜᴇ? The little tramp!" Oriane stamps her foot, stabbing into the loi berries I've served for breakfast. I couldn't resist serving the berries after last night.

By the time Zianne and Oriane arrived home very early this morning, I was already in bed, no trace of the servants, my makeup, or dress to be seen. Cyra had whisked them away, kissing my cheek and smiling so wide I felt sure her cheeks would ache all week.

"Who?" I ask, injecting a little bit of curiosity into my voice. I tell myself last night was a dream, that I was never

110

really there. It's the only way I'll be able to keep up the façade that I was here moping all night.

"The princess dancing with Jorai," Oriane seethes, her eyes blazing. "I've never seen her before."

"The conniving little thing was probably from some other poor, human-loving country looking for allies against Ellcombe," Stepmother scoffs. She's hardly touched her food this morning. "They'd probably benefit from having a proper fae king for once."

I barely manage to stifle the gasp before it's through my lips. It might not be treason to speak like that about a different country ... but it's close. Too close. Because such a figurative country that loves humans is more than a little similar to Ashennor.

But Zianne and Oriane are too absorbed in their discussion to notice me. Not entirely unusual, but I'm glad for it this time.

"No one knows who she was?" I finally ask.

"No! And I didn't even get one dance with Jorai because of her." Oriane lets out a long sigh. "But tonight will be different."

My heart gives a painful throb. She's not wrong. And though the thought threatens to dampen the joy that's been clinging to me all day, the memory of Jory is enough to hold it at bay.

Last night was more than I ever wanted. And it'll be enough to get me through the long years ahead in Zianne's service.

But even so, I can't stop the words from slipping through my lips. "Could I go tonight?"

Zianne laughs loud and long, the sound ringing out through the house.

"No, dear. You have nothing to wear, after all."

I pause. "Of course. You're right."

I scoop up their dirty dishes and return to the kitchen to wash up.

The morning passes in a happy blur. Oriane and Zianne grumble continuously about the 'princess' from last night, and they snap at me more than usual, but I hardly notice.

I hardly even hear them over the tune of our last dance whirling through my mind.

I barely see them through the image of Jorai's eyes holding my own.

Afternoon soon arrives and not even getting Oriane ready for the second night of the festival is enough to drag me back to reality. The dress I made for her is beyond anything I've ever made before. But it doesn't matter. Because I saw the way Jorai's eyes never even moved to her when she passed us last night.

Her words about a kiss the other night now seems nothing more than one of the many lies she spreads. Another entry in her journal of gossip.

I hold the dress as my stepsister steps into it and help her pull it up. The white fabric hugs her body, splitting right below the shoulder and all the way down to the hem.

It was quite a job to make sure the dress would sit right with the split, but stepping back, I can't deny it came out better than I expected. And the starlight gems in her hair just make it all the more beautiful.

"Kaylin!" Oriane squeals, jumping in place. Luckily, the dress doesn't move. "It's amazing!"

I smile, my eyes travelling over the dress again. You wouldn't catch me in it, but it really is amazing.

"Time to go, Oriane!"

Zianne walks past the room without sparing a glance our way. They're leaving incredibly early, but I wouldn't be surprised if people have already started arriving at the hill.

"Thank you, Kaylin." With one last smile, Oriane hurries after her mother, leaving me open mouthed with shock. It's a rare day that Oriane thanks me, and today of all days with her stewing over the princess last night ... I laugh.

I've only just packed up the work room—my mind dancing around the bonfire with Jorai—when a knock sounds at the entranceway and I jump. Did they forget something?

"Kaylin?" *Her* voice echoes through the house.

My eyes widen. "Cyra?"

No, no, no, no! She wasn't meant to come today. My ankle! I jump to my feet, hurrying across the room in search of something to hide it.

"Where are you?"

"Um, in here!" I call, dragging a long skirt I haven't finished sewing over my dress.

Cyra appears in the open archway just as I've got the skirt in place. The squeal she lets out is reminiscent of Oriane. "Oh, I just can't believe how beautiful you've grown!"

I blush. "I wasn't expecting you."

"I know." She waves her hand, hurrying over to grab my own. "But I just couldn't resist! And you know, Jorai will be disappointed if he doesn't see you." She wriggles her eyebrows. "He hasn't stopped talking about you."

"Really?" I can't help it. My heart jumps.

"Really. So, let's get you ready!"

"I don't know...."

"I'll have you back in time, just like last night." Her eyes turn pleading, and she pouts.

I purse my lips. I was home hours before Zianne last night.

"Oh, alright! What's one more night?"

Her squeal hurts my ears this time. But I feel lighter than I have in years.

"Good, because Jorai is going to fall over when he sees you!"

"What—?"

She hurries from the room, and I take the moment to hide my ankle even further, habit just as strong as any blood command.

Cyra hurries back into the room and I immediately straighten, but she doesn't seem to have noticed. In her arms is a golden dress that makes me gasp.

"Cyra, I can't wear that!" I splutter in disbelief.

"And why not?" She pouts again, crossing the room and laying the stunning gown on my worktable.

"But—but it's yours."

She raises her brow. "You wore one of mine last night."

"Yes, but this is—Cyra, look at it!" I gesture at the beautiful dress.

"I am, Kaylin. And I want you to wear it." She takes my hands in hers, giving them a squeeze. "I have so many years to make up for. Let me give you this one night." Her eyes are pleading, water swelling in them.

All I can manage is a nod.

A smile breaks out on her face. "Good, because I wasn't going to let you refuse."

Laughing, I turn my eyes back towards the dress, and my breath catches in my throat all over again. The russet gown from last night was the most beautiful thing I had ever seen up until today, and this more than surpasses it.

"Perhaps we can do without the disguise tonight?" Cyra asks, as she runs a hand over the dress.

My blood runs cold at her words. "No!" I clear my throat. "No. Zianne might see me. And Jorai … I'm human, Cyra."

"He wouldn't care," she says, turning to hold my eyes. "I don't care."

I swallow hard. "I can't."

"I know," she says, her shoulders slumping. I can tell it's the mention of Zianne and not Jorai that has convinced her. At least for now. Her face lights up again. "Oh, I can't wait for him to see you in this!"

"Did he really talk about me today?" I ask again, my heart stumbling.

Cyra gestures for me to take a seat and pulls out some makeup from inside her dress.

I sit, my eyes not leaving her face.

"He did." She plants a kiss on the top of my head and opens a small container to reveal a powder.

Cyra had promised to talk with me, to hear everything about my life, but I haven't had the time to work out what to say or how to hide what I really am.

Sitting here ... I need to start a conversation before she does. I smile. I know just what I want to talk about.

"Tell me about him. What have I missed?"

17

Jorai

WE'RE THE FIRST OF the guests to arrive at the hill. The organisers are still decorating, making sure the remnants of the previous night are gone, along with restocking the refreshments tables. The musicians are in their corner, tuning their instruments. And there are soldiers everywhere. Some in uniform, some dressed to blend in with the guests.

"The last of the men are moving into position now," Zephi explains. "They've been stationed along the road. We've doubled the guards at the entrance, and there will be more within tonight's crowd, both in uniform and casual dress."

Looking around, I can see what he means. There are maybe fifty men wandering around, barely a fraction of the number of fae and humans attending tonight. But it's more than we've had on duty in a long time. "The rebels would be fools to try anything."

Zephi nods, looking out over the city sprawled below us glinting in the afternoon light. "Leave it to me, Jorai. You just find that girl."

"You're as bad as Cyra," I laugh, but a rush of gratitude hits me. I just can't get this girl from my mind. "Thanks, Zeph."

"It's been a long time since you couldn't get your eyes off a girl," he remarks.

I chuckle. "Does it count when you're eight years old?"

Zephi turns serious eyes on me. "Yes."

I smile but force myself not to think of who he means. She's long gone, taken somewhere else by her father after her mother died. She might not even remember me. Ten years is a long time for a human.

"The first guests are arriving," Zephi says, his demeanour changing immediately. His back straightens and his shoulders widen, looking more the part of a guard. Zephi bows, then hurries away.

My eyes study the hidden faces of every blonde woman that arrives. A thought occurs to me ... would I even recognise her tonight?

These countless guests are all in new dresses and masks; even the men like myself are in new tunics and jackets or cloaks. But I could never forget *her*. I stare into the eyes of every blonde woman, watch their lips for a hint of a smile, but none of them are her.

I might not know her name, but I could never forget those eyes. One woman blushes under the intensity of my stare, and I force myself to turn away.

"You'll find her," I whisper under my breath. It feels as though a part of me is missing without her.

The music weaves around us as I mingle with my guests. I greet face after face, but always my eyes are pulled away as another woman arrives, and always my heart sinks.

I'm forced to greet the next and the next and the next. The music soon morphs into a cheerful tune, and people begin to amble towards the bonfire again, some alone, some in pairs, right as Oriane appears before me again.

I barely hold in my sigh, but I still plaster on the smile of a dutiful prince.

"Oriane," I greet, unsure whether I should look below her eyes and to the dress she's wearing tonight.

"Prince Jorai." She smiles, and starlight glints in her hair. "I didn't think things could get any better than last night." Oriane looks around, taking in the decorations and the people dancing. "You've outdone yourself."

"Thank you, although I didn't do anything."

She laughs, reaching out to take my hand. "So modest. But this is all for you!"

I frown, subtly trying to pull my hand away from her. She gives no sign that she's noticed, though I manage to break free. "It was—"

"Could I have this first dance?" she asks, looking up at me through her lashes. At my crown.

This woman is determined. And she hasn't stopped breaking protocol.

I force a smile. "I need to greet my guests."

Her eyes seem to flicker, but she just smiles. "Of course, maybe later?"

"I already have a partner for the night."

I don't hang around to give her another chance to bid for my attention. Instead, I walk directly over to the entrance-way and join the guards, greeting the two court members that have arrived.

The guards cast me curious glances but say nothing. I wasn't supposed to join them, since they are meant to verify everyone before letting them in, but there is something about Oriane that makes me want to steer clear of her. She seems nice enough, but it feels like it's fake. Oriane presents her court face to me, but I know nothing about what she's really like.

But the girl—I really need to learn her name—she feels *real*. I laugh despite myself, earning a puzzled glance from the guards. But I can't help it. She feels real in a way no one else has before. Like she's actually seeing *me*.

My grin widens, not seeing the man I'm greeting. How can someone feel real when I don't even know her name? But I can't explain it in any other way. That girl ... I need to find her again.

My eyes travel over the heads of those lining up to enter. I still can't see her. My heart sinks further with every face that isn't hers. But maybe she's just late?

There's a loud clang from across the hill, and people are shouting and screaming. My stomach drops. The rebels can't be here? My sword is in my hand in an instant.

I push through the crowd, fighting against people running both to and from the disturbance. Dusk is starting to settle, and though the fae can still see clearly, the humans can't even with the fires. Their panic shows as they stumble away.

I glimpse soldiers gathered in a circle and finally break through the masses. "What's happening? I demand.

Zephi disengages from the group and speaks loudly and clearly, and I know the words aren't really for me. "Nothing to worry about, just someone who got a little carried away."

"The rebels?" I ask quietly as he joins me.

He nods, his eyes sweeping over the scene. "We caught two of them. It looks like a third got away."

"What were they doing?"

"Setting up some kind of contraption. Looks like it was going to blow up the refreshments and the musicians."

My stomach drops at the thought.

I follow his gaze. The soldiers must be hiding the contraption from view, and the only other sign of the disturbance is the large silver tray on the ground and the soft golden treats that have been strewn across the grass.

Things could have been so much worse.

I resist the urge to run a hand through my hair, looking around. "Escort them to the palace dungeon. Was anyone hurt?"

"No, everything's fine. Taavi noticed them before anything could happen."

I knew it was a good idea to have him on duty. "Very well. Then let's deal with this as quickly as possible and get back to it."

My captain holds my gaze, approval in his eyes, then starts issuing orders as I turn back towards the crowd.

"Just a little misunderstanding," I say, trying to calm the throng of people staring at our little scene. "As the captain said, just someone who got a little carried away."

At my words, the musicians start up another song, and slowly the crowd begins to disperse and couples return to dancing.

"Well handled," Raiden's voice sounds in my ear.

"There you are!" I remark with a grin.

He shrugs. "I had to wait for my escort to arrive." He smiles self-deprecatingly. I know how ridiculous it seems. Raiden hardly needs one, given his years of experience as a soldier in Frigarth. But he's an ambassador now, and we have protocols to follow.

"I'm sorry," I say anyway.

"Can't be helped." He shrugs again, glancing around the party. "Have you seen Cyra? I got roped into promising another dance. She's keen on the faster beats."

"No. I doubt she's even here. She takes a while to get ready. Says it's all her hair."

I scan the crowd looking, for once not for the girl, but for my father. He should have come to find out what was happening by now. But it seems he still hasn't arrived.

I purse my lips. He only appeared for a couple hours last night before leaving.

I suppose I shouldn't be surprised now. But I thought he would at least try to take the threats by the rebels seriously. Never mind that it's my birthday, too.

"I'd better get an update on my father," I say with a sigh.

I'm pushing through the crowd before Raiden responds. The man sees much, but this is one thing I don't want him to see in me. Though I'm sure he's already realised my relationship with my father is strained at times. I push the thoughts away. Zephi is busy with the soldiers, so I search for one of the guards. They should know what's happening.

My eyes land on a woman Zephi's age, with dark green eyes and long, curly hair pulled back from her face. "Litta!"

She alters course, straightening her uniform as she joins me. Twin daggers sit fastened at her hips. We allow our warriors to choose their own standard weapons, though they must be experts in the sword. "Prince Jorai."

"Do you have any news of my father?" I ask.

"He's not due to arrive for another hour, Your Highness."

"Oh." Typical. "Have a message sent to him about what's happened here."

She bows, merging back into the crowd. But at that moment there's a low ripple throughout the fae and humans already gathered, and murmurs and whispers seem to assault my ears in a low buzz.

My head whips around, following their gazes and all thought of the rebels has left me.

The breath seems to leave my lungs, and I know I'm grinning like a fool, but I can't stop. She's here.

18

Kaylin

"What's happening, Geralt?" I ask as the man rounds the carriage.

"I'm not sure, my lady. There's some kind of disturbance over by the refreshments."

I fiddle with the skirt of my dress, chewing my lip. "Do you think it's OK to attend?"

He pauses, turning to scan the hilltop. "They're already returning to the celebrations, lady. I don't believe there is anything to fear."

I don't correct him in assuming that's why I'm worried. My thoughts had turned to Zianne and Oriane as the absurd notion that perhaps they knew I was coming occurred to me.

But there's no way they could know. Cyra arrived after they'd left. But that sharp pang of anxiety hangs on, nonetheless. I shouldn't be doing this.

"Are you ready, miss?" My driver's soft green eyes are on mine, a move I have often regretted with my owners. The ease with which he looks at me tells me more than enough about his own experience as a human. He doesn't suffer for looking at the fae. Has never been hit or punished by magic for simply holding their eyes.

"Yes. I'm sorry, Geralt." I take his hand, using the other to carefully lift my skirt enough not to trip but still not too high.

"Would you escort me inside, Geralt?" I ask.

I don't know what Cyra has told him about me—whether he knows I'm human or thinks I'm fae—but the older man's eyebrows rise in surprise.

I smile. "I know you're here for me, but you can enjoy the night too."

He pauses, as though thinking it over. Then, finally, he smiles, holding out his arm for me. "Thank you, my lady."

Geralt stays by my side as we approach the guards standing by the arch. His face betrays nothing, no sign of nerves, as we're halted. My own fingers tighten on his arm, but he doesn't even blink.

"Invitation?" a fae woman with a spear clasped in one hand asks.

I pull a crumpled piece of parchment from the folds of my dress. Cyra had come beyond prepared today. Armed with the information that security had been tightened, she'd written up an invitation for me under a false name.

I glance over my shoulder as the woman scans the invitation. Cyra shouldn't be too far away. She only stepped out of the carriage just out of sight of the hilltop.

"All clear." The woman hands me the parchment, this time letting her eyes travel over my dress. The shine of it seems to reflect in her eyes.

Geralt kindly waits for me to take the first step forwards, then easily keeps pace with me. I'm scanning the crowd, but it looks like he was right. Everyone's slowly returning to the festivities. People are dancing around the bonfire again, though there still seems to be a small cluster over where the tables were last night.

But as we come to a stop, a low buzz seems to rise among the crowd.

"I'll leave you here, lady." He releases my arm, bowing. "As last night, I will find you when it is time to go."

"Thank you. Enjoy the festival."

He's already turned away, but he glances back, and his eyes seem to shine with excitement. It makes him seem years younger. Sadness hits me at the thought that I won't see this kind man again after tonight.

My neck prickles, the hair rising as the feeling that I'm being watched settles over me. I smooth the front of my dress and scan the many faces, but it quickly becomes clear that everyone is watching me. Murmurs rise up among them, both fae and human faces alike turned my way.

I feel my cheeks heat and instinctively raise a hand to my golden-feathered mask, reassuring myself that it's still in place.

Perhaps I should have protested harder at Cyra's insistence to wear this dress. It's worth more than I could ever hope to earn, or pay off Zianne, in a lifetime. My shoulders are covered in soft golden laced sleeves, with silver-grey feathers sown into the fabric.

The dress hugs my torso tightly, like a corset, but spreads out from my abdomen in a wide arch, spreading down to the ground, covering the flat shoes I insisted on wearing so that I had some chance of walking tonight. But the skirt is covered with swan feathers, ranging from gold, through to silver, and then to white. Some are embroidered, while others are real.

It's clearly designed for Cyra, after her shifted form, and I look like a princess. Maybe I should go before either Oriane or Zianne sees me.

My hand is still pressed to my mask, my cheeks still flushed with warmth, when a flash of ice-blue eyes appear, and I'm drawn to them. My feet are taking me forwards against my will, and all the arguments I'd formed seem to vanish in an instant.

Cyra's words repeat in my mind, stories of the years I've missed. Everyday moments that I wish I had been there for. My hand drops from my face, as I find myself looking up into Jorai's eyes.

My heart skips a beat at what I see there so clearly displayed.

A flicker of electricity seems to run through them.

"Hello," I murmur.

"You—" he stammers, then clears his throat and tries again, but he can't seem to get more than one word out. "You—"

"Thank you."

He grins, his eyes travelling over me again, then lingering on my face. "I've never seen anything like you."

My already warm cheeks suddenly feel on fire. "I've never worn anything like this."

"No," he says, shaking his head. "I mean *you.*"

The eyes of everyone gathered are still on us, and I know that means both Zianne and Oriane are looking on, but in this moment, I can't summon the composure to care.

"You're quite something yourself." I run a hand down the front of his jacket before I know what I'm doing. Wait. I snatch it back, but he doesn't notice. What am I doing? I can't—*we* can't.

His hand finds mine. "Dance with me again."

And, curse my weakness, I do. Just one night, I tell myself as he leads me back to that silver bonfire. Just one more night of bliss and that will be it.

I'll purge him from my mind.

I'll never think of him again.

Even if he takes my heart with him. Just one more night.

We enter the throng mid-song, but it's like we've been dancing together our whole lives.

Everything fades and it's just us. Just the two of us on this hilltop, twirling around the bonfire in one large loop. His eyes are on mine, my hand in his. My face hurts from grinning and laughing. And I never want it to end.

As the song finishes, we come to a stop, clapping along with those around us. A finger taps my shoulder. Hard.

"I don't suppose I could cut in?"

I stiffen, stepping out of Jorai's arms to find Oriane staring hungrily at the prince. She doesn't spare me a glance.

"I'm sorry, Oriane," Jorai says firmly, but his fingers brush mine. "I told you before, I'm taken."

She sucks in a deep breath, the kind she usually takes before erupting into a rage, and I take an unconscious step backwards. But with what must have been a supreme effort of will, Oriane smiles. "My apologies."

I watch her retreating figure all the way across the hilltop and through the entrance arch. My heart thunders in my chest the entire time. She didn't notice. She doesn't know. It's fine. It's OK.

"Love?" Jorai's voice draws me back, and I manage to summon a smile.

He returns it, but his eyes are fixed on me again as he steps closer.

"I feel as though I should know you," he whispers, his breath tickling my skin, "but I could never forget someone like you."

"Perhaps another dance will help?" I offer him my hand, the other going to his shoulder, forcing another smile.

"I doubt you'll tell me, then?" he says softly.

I turn my eyes down. This could never be. "No."

His rough fingers gently lift my chin. "Then another dance it is. We'll dance until I worm a name out of you."

"Then we'll be dancing a long, long time."

"I fail to see a downside to that," he says, slipping a hand to my hip and pulling me back into the fray.

We pause for drinks, and sometime during the night Jorai loses his jacket, revealing a stunning tunic threaded with vines.

"Oh!" Cyra's voice practically screams from behind me. "I love your dress!"

I spin, nearly spilling my drink, to find my godmother bouncing on her toes, her green eyes twinkling. I flare my eyes at her in a what-do-you-think-you're-doing way.

She winks.

"Aunt Cyra! This is," Jorai pauses, flashing me a grin, "well, I'm yet to get her name from her. But this is the girl I was telling you about."

Her smile widens. "It's so nice to meet you," she says, gingerly pulling me into a hug so as not to damage the feathers of my dress. "Are you sure you can't tell him?" she whispers in my ear, low enough that I have to strain to hear her.

"Not tonight. Zianne," I whisper back, my heart breaking into a pounding race. She wouldn't tell him, surely?

Cyra raises her voice again. "Jorai hasn't stopped talking about you all day."

She pulls back, thankfully maintaining our illusion.

I glance at Jorai, my pulse settling once more, but he nods unashamedly.

"That's very sweet, my lady."

"I hope you'll tell us all soon where you've been hiding."

At a loss for what to say, my mouth opens and closes. Of course she'd say that, unaware of what I am. Maybe she can look past the fact that I'm a human, she would even be outraged that I'm a slave, but Jorai and the rest of the court would be horrified. Disgusted.

"Alright, Cyra, don't scare her off," Jorai laughs, saving me from lying.

"Have you seen Raiden around here?" Cyra asks, looking around. "That man knows how to dance."

Jorai shakes his head, and I happily return to picking at the food table. "I saw him right at the start, but not since."

"I wonder why," Cyra says wryly. "Oh, well. Perhaps this fine young man will dance with me?"

"Can't, Cyra. I'm on duty," the captain's deep voice rumbles from behind me. "Is this her?"

I swallow the bite of cake I'd just taken. "Does everyone know about me?"

Jorai smiles ruefully, but Zephi and Cyra merely grin.

"Yes," the captain says simply. "It's nice to properly meet you."

I know he's thinking of last night when he took Jorai's jacket during one of our dances. His face betrays nothing of a deeper recognition, but I'm no longer worried about that. I'm safe in anonymity tonight. And even with the weight of metal still on my ankle, it's freeing.

"You too, Captain."

"Oh, I love this song!" Cyra turns to Zephi, pouting. "Please? Just one."

With a dramatic sigh, Zephi nods. "One, Cyra. Only one."

I laugh as he leads her away, and turn to Jorai. "Let's join them."

It's like some giant puppeteer has taken over the couples as they all begin to move together as one. I glance around nervously. I don't know this dance. I don't really know any dances. What we've done so far was hardly choreographed.

"Don't worry." Jorai pulls me closer, so close that my chest bumps his, and I swear I can feel his heart beating in time with my own. "I know this one."

The music swells, and the prince leads me on. We twirl, step, swing, dip, and sway, and then as one, every man in the group swings their partner out and the women swirl away, stopping before a new partner.

Zephi looks down at me, seeming to tower over me. Even though he is only slightly taller than Jorai, he is still over a foot taller than my small frame. But the captain offers me a slight bow as he takes my hand in his. His dark eyes study me. "You don't know this dance, little swan?"

"No," I say, blinking at the nickname as he guides me on. His steps are as flawless as Jorai's.

As I pass under his arm in a gentle spin, his voice carries down to me, softly. "Why is it that you hide who you are?"

My feet stumble, tangled in my dress, but Zephi steadies me, leading me into the next move as though nothing has happened. I attempt to gather my scrambled thoughts. I don't want to lie to this man. Nor do I think he would believe me if I did.

But I can't say nothing at all. Yes, this is a masquerade dance, but that is no real excuse.

"I—I don't want to hurt him," I finally say, looking up into his angular face. Perhaps my words have a double meaning in answer to his question, but both are the truth.

His gaze studies my face. "I believe that."

And then I'm twirling back towards Jorai, who catches me in his arms like he'll never let me go again.

"Was that as dreadful for you as it was for me?" he whispers against my ear.

"Yes." I laugh.

His eyes trail over my lips. "Laugh again for me."

"Why?" I let go of him briefly to adjust the sleeve of my dress.

"Because it's the most beautiful sound in the world."

I blush. "I will only if you will."

"Deal."

And we're laughing together like absolute fools as we leap and spin around the bonfire and nothing could be better than this.

My chest is heaving when the dance ends and the music seamlessly moves into a new, slower song. But I don't step back. I don't let go of him, but rather slip my hands up to his shoulders.

"Tell me your name," he murmurs.

"I can't." I fix my eyes on his chest, not daring to look up into his face. The face I would have told anything to as a child.

"Why not?"

I shake my head. Tears are welling in my eyes. I would like nothing more than to tell him. For him to finally see *me*. But

I have a debt to pay off; I'm a slave, a human. And he's my prince.

"Love, tell me. Tell me your name."

"No!" I draw back, though not enough to leave his arms. Even now, I can't bring myself to leave him.

"What's stopping you?" His voice is rough. Worried. Like he thinks I could be in trouble. Or maybe I don't love him.

My heart stutters. But the realisation bounces around my head. I love him.

Fire flares in my veins. Not at him, but at how unfair this is. And then I'm yelling at him.

"You can't know! You can't ever know because then you'd see this can never be more than a dream. I don't want it to end, Jory!"

"What—" the words die on his lips, and his blue eyes widen.

I'm backtracking, running over what I've said because that's recognition lighting in his eyes, and that's my name his lips are forming.

And then the world falls apart.

19

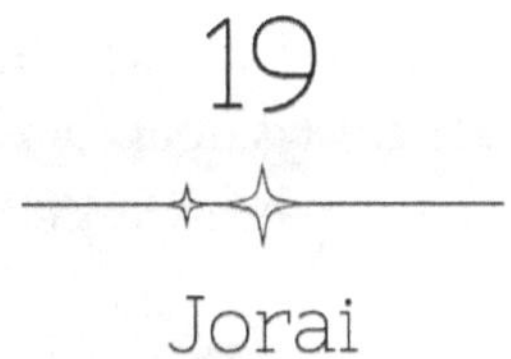

Jorai

ELECTRICITY RUNS ALONG THE ground, missing every set of feet in a true feat of skill, but kicking up dust that instantly whips around us.

An explosion sounds somewhere behind me. Or is it in front? I whirl around, panicked bodies knocking into me, and in that moment, I feel her small body tugged from my arms.

"Kaylin!" Dust runs down my throat, and I heave great, hacking coughs. Screams echo around the hilltop. A large figure slams into me and I go sprawling, landing on something soft and small. Shoving a hand under my back, I draw out a small, black shoe.

But that's not all that the ground reveals as the dust settles. There are deep rivets in the grass, like someone was dragged, like someone fought. No. No, that doesn't make sense.

Shoving the shoe in my belt, I'm on my feet in an instant, my sword in my hand. "Kaylin!"

I dive into the panicking crowd, looking into every face. Searching for hers through the dust and dirt clogging the air. How did I not recognise her? How could I look into those eyes and not know?

"Kaylin!"

My own name rises above the screams, but I ignore it. Zephi will find me. He always does. It's Kaylin that I need to find. The girl who had my heart as a child and never truly gave it back.

"Kaylin!"

"Jorai!" A hand closes on my shoulder. "We need to get you out of here, Your Highness."

"No." I wrench free from my friend's grip, running a hand through my hair. "I need to find her. I need to find Kaylin." I can hear the plea in my voice, but I don't care. All I do is try to rein in my panic a little. I need a clear head.

"Kaylin?" His brow furrows, and I will his mind to catch up. "The maid's daughter?"

"Yes!"

His eyes light with understanding. "The swan. We'll look together, Jor. Do not leave my side."

We plunge on even as the crowd begins to thin, as the screams slowly dissipate, until there's no one left. No guests, no musicians, and no Kaylin.

·)⟩⟩●⟨⟨·

"I have to go find her!" My palms slam into the oak desk.

"Watch. Your. Tone." In the king's voice is a deadly warning, but for once I don't listen to it.

"We can't just leave her to the rebels!" I gesture wildly through the archway, as though the rebels are out there hiding among the flowers and hedges.

I almost wish they were so that I could tear them apart.

My father's ice-blue eyes are thoughtful, and a shadow passes over them.

"Eran—"

He shoots Cyra a quelling look. If I could think above the pounding of my blood in my ears, I might wonder about the terror in her eyes, about the tracks through the grime on her cheeks. But I can't spare her a thought right now.

"There is nothing to be done," my father decides, leaning back in his chair. He meets my eyes, and there isn't a hint of remorse in them. "Once they realise she's a human, they'll have no reason to keep her alive, Jorai. The girl's already dead."

"What? Father, you can't—I can't—"

"I can and *you* will." My father rises to his feet, his voice booming through the room. "You are not to go looking for this human. I forbid it."

"Jorai," Cyra says, taking my arm in a steel-like grip. "Your father's right."

Rounding on her, about to say something I know I'll regret, the words die on my lips. Hidden from my father by my own form, Cyra is gazing up into my face with a look that says something completely different to what her words did. Finally, her tearstained face penetrates. She wouldn't cry for the festival ... Are these for Kaylin?

I let my shoulders slump, but I hold her meaningful gaze, hoping she'll answer the question, the hope, I know shows in my own eyes. She gives a tiny, almost imperceptible nod.

"Fine," I say, injecting as much resignation into my voice as I can as I turn back to my father. "You're right."

Zephi shifts beside me, but I don't dare catch his eye.

My father nods, a satisfied smirk tilting his lips. "I'm sorry these scum have ruined your birthday festivities, but I think we can risk continuing tomorrow."

The words are like a stab to my heart. He really thinks that I care about the festival?

"I look forward to it. In the meantime, I'd like to learn what we can from the rebels we caught. If we're lucky, we might make a few more arrests." I force the words through my lips, trying to maintain some semblance of calm.

"Ah." My father sits heavily back in his chair. "I'm afraid that won't be possible. They're no longer here."

"What?" My one chance to find her, gone.

His eyebrows rise, but he glances at Cyra and Zephi, the only others in the room. "Leave us."

I don't turn as they go, but stare down at my father. What is this expression on his face? What is it that he's hiding?

As Cyra and Zephi's footsteps fade down the hall, my father speaks in a low tone. "The men caught earlier tonight weren't real rebels."

"But they were setting up an explo—"

"It wasn't real." He waves his hand dismissively. "I hired them."

My stomach drops. "You hired them?"

But it's disgust, not surprise that settles over me in the wake of his admission. And that makes it so much worse.

"Don't look at me like that," he snaps. "With Frigarth breathing down our necks and these threats coming in regularly, we needed something to calm them down!"

"So you paid some men to blow up the festival?"

"No," his voice booms. "I paid some men to make us look good. No one was going to get hurt."

"Except someone did," I say, my blood boiling.

Kaylin is out there and I have no way of finding her now but that's not something he cares about. I need to find something he does.

I straighten my back, staring him down. "And now we look even worse. You might not care about what's happened tonight, but catching the rebels who did this is exactly what we need. And if I get the chance to do it, I'll take it."

He doesn't say anything as I turn on my heel and leave.

"Jorai!" Cyra whisper-shouts from a room to my left, two halls away from my father's office.

I duck into the room, only to find Zephi there as well.

"You know something, don't you?" I ask my aunt, looking into her pained eyes. "You knew it was her."

"Yes," she says. Her eyes well, but the tears don't fall. Instead, she thrusts her shoulders back. "Kaylin is my goddaughter. I didn't know where she was all these years, but I found her yesterday. She's back with the family her father used to serve."

"Goddaughter?" An echo of her words to Raiden come back to me, *I've been looking for my goddaughter and her father for some time, but with no luck.* Cyra's goddaughter was a human. Kaylin.

She nods, her eyes daring me to rebuke her, but I could never. "Her mother and I couldn't tell anyone who I was to them back then. No one would have accepted it. Even when the law changed, Eran wouldn't have supported it."

"I know," I whisper. I remember the way Kaylin used to cling to Cyra when we were alone. It was my aunt who introduced us, after all. I never gave it a second thought as a child. It was just how they were. But never in front of anyone else.

"But why—?" I can't bring myself to finish the question, but Cyra knows what I mean instantly.

"She didn't want you to know it was her in case Zianne found out she went to the festival when she wasn't allowed to go."

I close my eyes, and nod. There's no time to linger on decisions already made. "How are we going to find her?"

A flash of memory hits me.

I perk up. "Who was the man who escorted Kaylin at the festival?"

Cyra shakes her head. "Geralt. I asked him to look after her; he's a servant here. He won't know anything."

Zephi clears his throat, stopping me from responding. From spiralling.

"The rebels who escaped aren't the only ones we caught, Your Highness," Zephi says, his words washing over me like a cool balm.

My mouth drops open. "There's another?"

He nods.

"The rebels from earlier weren't real," I say bitterly. "My father hired them."

Cyra gasps, her hands flying to her mouth. "That bastard!"

"Never mind that." I turn to Zephi, more determined than ever. "Does my father know about the rebel you caught?"

"I have not had a chance to tell him." His eyes glint. The Captain of the Royal Guards, my captain, risks treason in this moment. And I will never stop thanking him.

"Then let's go."

A dark staircase leading down to the dungeons gapes open in the wall ahead of us, and my stomach twists. I hate the dungeons. Every fae does. It's fully enclosed down there, and the only light sources are whatever the guards bring with them on their rounds. The starlight ends at the top of the stairs, and regular dark stones are used instead. Not even they will provide a source of illumination.

I turn to my aunt. Her eyes are fixed on the stairwell, and a barely supressed shudder ripples through her. "Wait here," I order.

"Why?" She tilts her chin up defiantly.

"Because I'm not going to ask kindly, and we need some-one to distract the king."

She pauses, then nods.

Zeph grabs the torch left lit in a bracket to the side, and we descend into the shadows. My skin crawls with every step further away from the light.

"Open up," Zephi calls as we reach the gate at the bottom of the long staircase. A fae guard's face appears, pale and flickering in the firelight. The shifts down here are short, no more than three hours. It'd be cruel to make them stay much longer than that.

The gate clicks, swinging open with a long, eerie creak. We duck through, and the gate clangs shut behind us. I resist the urge to shudder.

"This way." Even Zephi's voice is thick with displeasure as it rings out in the darkness.

The rebel has been left deep inside the dungeons. We turn left, right, then left again, past empty cell after empty cell. There aren't many prisoners down here. A traitor or two from years past, maybe a murderer, but the thought of this eternal darkness is enough to discourage most from crime.

Zephi finally draws us to a halt.

"Faina?" The surprise in my voice bounces around the close walls, echoing back at me. This can't be right.

The lithe woman jolts where she is curled up in a corner and jumps to her feet. Tears have left rivers down her face, and her short brown hair is already a mess.

"Your Highness!" she gasps, racing forwards to grip the bars of the cell. "There's been some kind of mistake! Please, I don't belong in here."

I glance at Zephi, but his face is stony. "There has been no mistake."

I don't second-guess my captain's words.

"But there has! Please! My brother must be worried sick."

"Where was Armis tonight?" I hardly recognise my voice. Good.

"At—at the festival," she sobs, "like everyone else."

"Perhaps we should send someone out to retrieve him as well?"

"No! No, Your Highness."

"Are you saying he wasn't involved?"

Her shoulders droop. "No, he wasn't."

"Then you need to give me something, Faina."

A strange glint enters her eyes, but it's gone in a heartbeat. Perhaps it was the torch playing tricks. "They took her into the forest, by the old ruins."

I'm running back through the corridors as soon as the last word is through her lips.

I'm coming, Kaylin.

20

Jorai

Z EPHI, A HANDFUL OF carefully chosen guards, and I slink through the darkness, weaving silently between the trees. The ruins aren't far into the forest, but they offer shelter and a safe place to lie low. The ideal place for the rebels to hide while things die down.

I'm coming. I'm coming. The words circle my mind, as if by repeating them over and over they might somehow reach her. Comfort her in this darkness.

The river sounds in my ears, a soft trickle this time of year, no more than a creek really. We're close.

I glance at Zephi, nodding. He silently gestures for the men to spread out, getting ready to encircle the ruins of the little home.

I force myself to take quiet and shallow breaths, but fear makes it hard.

What will we find? What if my father is right? What if they realised they don't need her?

A stone pillar appears in the darkness, vines and moss growing up it, great tufts of grass at the base. We're here.

Zephi lets out one loud, long whistle, and we rush forwards.

Only to find ... nothing.

Nothing at all.

The ruins are empty, devoid of any sign of recent visitors. Grasses and seedlings have sprouted up between the stone pavers. They show no sign of being trampled under the feet of many, or even one, fae.

Faina lied. The realisation is like a blow to my heart.

The air grows heavy, my hair stands on end, and wind begins to whip up.

"Jorai," Zephi murmurs in warning.

My heart is thundering. I haven't lost control of my magic like this in years. But magic feeds off emotion, and right now, I can't seem to get a grip on mine. Electricity begins to roll across the ground. Startled shouts rise among the guards as they stumble back.

"Jorai!" Zephi grabs me roughly, heedless of the charge of my own body as he spins me to face him. "We will find her. But you need to get this under control."

I nod, the air still crackling.

His other hand grips my shoulder and suddenly I am a child again. Learning how to control this gift for the first time. "Deep breath in through your nose, out through your mouth."

In and out, I breathe. Over and over, feeling the magic prickling over my skin, through my veins. The electricity dies, the wind settles, and slowly, the air begins to lighten.

He nods affirmingly. "Good."

"What are we going to do?" I drop my head in defeat.

"We're going back to the palace to speak with Cyra. Maybe she can tell us more about Kaylin."

"But what good is—" My breath catches. "Raiden. We need Raiden."

21

Kaylin

A HIGH-PITCHED RINGING IN my ears is the first thing that I notice. It feels both like it's been there forever and yet only just started as I slowly claw back to consciousness.

My head throbs, and a sticky substance has dried down the length of my face. Shifting, something coarse pulls at my wrists, digging into my skin. I groan, blinking my eyes open in the cold darkness.

Air catches in my throat as the room comes into focus. I've never seen anything like it amongst the fae. Because it looks like I'm underground. The closest I've ever seen is my little root cellar bedroom. It's a large dark-stoned room, empty aside from me. There's a solid wooden door in the wall to my right. There are no windows. No lights except for a small flame by the door, which flickers dangerously like it will go out at any moment.

The air is stuffy, old, and damp. A tiny gap, no bigger than my fist, in the wall opposite me proves to be the only source of fresh air. And I doubt I'm getting much at all.

But it's not the room itself that has a scream building in my lungs. It's *me*.

I'm seated in the centre of the room, my arms tied behind me with a rope. My legs are free, but there's nothing I can do anyway. If I could even get to my feet, the rickety chair would come with me. The cold stone under one of my feet tells me I've lost a shoe. And feathers from my dress are strewn across the dirty floor.

My mouth opens unbidden to scream for help, but what if whoever grabbed me hears? What if there's no one to hear me at all?

I take the chance.

"Help! Somebody, help me!"

My voice echoes back at me.

"Hello? Please, is anyone there?" I call out.

Tears well in my eyes. No one would bother to look for me. Zianne and Oriane wouldn't care. And Jorai ... I shove the thought away. He wouldn't want me now. Not now that he knows who I am.

"Please!"

But no one is coming. No one is going to help me. Just as the thought settles itself deep inside of me, the door clicks and slowly opens.

My brow furrows. "Ori—"

"Did you have a nice sleep, princess?"

I snap my mouth closed, and stare at my stepsister in confusion. What is happening right now? Oriane struts forwards, making room for Armis and a man I don't recognise.

But none of them seem to know who I am. My mask is still in place, my ears and ankles covered, and I'm wearing a dress worth more than my own life. I press my lips together. Do I try to let her know it's me? That I'm not whoever it is they think I am? But something tells me I'm in more danger than ever.

Oriane comes to a halt in front of me, looking down with open disdain. She's no longer in the dress I made her for the festival. How long have I been here?

"If you cooperate, everything will be fine. We have to rough you up a little of course, so they know we're serious. But you'll be back home in whatever little worthless kingdom you came from just as soon as Jorai stops this childish campaign for the humans."

My lips press firmer together, my mind racing. The dinner at Zianne's house. My eyes close. They're the rebels. They're the ones who've been threatening Jorai.

But the prince won't come for me, not now that he knows who I am.

And what will happen to me when they realise this was all for nothing?

22

Jorai

"Did you find her?" Cyra shoots to her feet, running forwards. But I don't need to tell her; she can already see the answer in my eyes. "No, no, no! Let me speak to the rebel."

The intensity of her words nearly makes me stumble backwards. I've never, *never*, seen my aunt angry. And this goes beyond. Her face is stony, pure hatred flashing in her eyes.

"There's no point," I say, though a part of me would love to unleash her on Faina. "It's you we need to talk to."

"Me?" At this, she deflates a little.

"You," I say, then gesture over my shoulder as I hear Raiden arrive. "And him."

"I admit, I'm curious to know what this is about." The ambassador crosses the room, his eyes carefully flickering between us. He knows about the attack, of course, how could he not? But the look he's giving me makes me wonder if he already knows it was a human taken.

"I need your help finding her," I say. I'll beg if I have to, but if I'm right about this man, he won't make me.

He tilts his head. "The human."

"Yes."

He grunts. "And is it true your father forbade you?"

My eyebrows rise. "How could you know that?"

"He's not being very secretive about it." Approval shines in his eyes. "I suggest we make this quick. Before he changes his mind about not actively stopping you."

With no time for polished words, I throw it out there. "I was blind. I ignored your concerns, and I even ignored my captain when he told me what I didn't want to believe. But the rebels won't keep Kaylin alive for long once they realise she's a human. Help us find her."

The ambassador may not have found his princess yet, but that doesn't mean he isn't one of the most skilled trackers in all of Ashennor right now.

"Right," he says, as though he was simply waiting for me to ask. "Tell me about her."

"Her mother used to work as a maid here when we were kids. Kaylin used to come with her all the time. But I hadn't seen her in years until last night. Her mother died, and we'd heard her father moved them away." I glance at Cyra.

"My goddaughter," Cyra explains and understanding lights in Raiden's eyes, "came back to the house Maaz worked at. She's a servant there."

"Then we'll go there first. We need to know all we can about her."

Zianne's estate is large and sprawling. A beautifully tended garden lines the front road, gleaming in the early dawn. Kaylin's hands tilled this earth, cared for these flowers. Everywhere I look are signs of the life she's led here, without me. *I'm coming, Kaylin.*

Our company halts at the entrance to the house, the horses pawing at the ground as though they can feel the restlessness in my bones. Cyra, Zephi, Raiden and I dismount, leaving the two guards that accompanied us to watch the horses.

"Hello?" I call from the entranceway, hardly managing to stop myself from barging in.

There is no response from the darkness, and a hollowness seems to hang over the building.

"Something's not right," Cyra whispers beside me. I glance down at her, the fear and foreboding settling over me reflected in her own eyes.

I walk inside.

"Jorai, wait!"

But I don't wait for my captain, leading the way into the deserted building myself. The echoes of soft footsteps behind me tells me my three companions are following.

Starlight reflects back at me from nearly every room. From tables, pillars, and clothing. We check everywhere. But there is no sign of anyone.

Poking my head into a small room down to the right reveals a space filled to the brim with material, buttons, jewels, pins, and half-finished dresses. The room is thick with Kaylin's scent, and I can't stop the smile that comes to my lips. Her mother used to love making clothing. We'd play together at her feet, as she and Cyra exchanged gossip.

"She worked in here?" Raiden's voice jolts me from my thoughts.

"Yes," Cyra says even as I nod. It's imperative Raiden gets as much information as he can. "She made dresses for Zianne and her daughter."

"Does anyone else live here?" he inquires.

"I don't think so." Cyra's voice is uncertain. "Lael, Zianne's husband, died before Kaylin was born."

It's unusual for the fae to remarry. Once we've found our one, our hearts remain theirs forever.

"We need to keep searching." Zephi's voice sounds from the doorway; he's the only one who hasn't entered the workroom. There's barely anywhere to stand inside. We shuffle out, looking around the empty house.

"Let's split up," Raiden says. "Call out anything that might tell us more about Kaylin."

My feet lead me further into the house, bypassing room after room. None of them feel like Kaylin, though I'm sure it's her hands that have kept this place immaculate, and I realise as I pass a sitting room that it is her room I'm searching for. At the end of the house is a kitchen, screened off from a dining room and sitting room.

My footsteps echo as I peek around the screen. Nothing. What is going on here? Surely Zianne and Oriane would have returned home by now. With the festival long over and the rebels on the loose, surely, they would want to get somewhere safe?

I'm just about to head back to find one of the others when my eyes land on a staircase leading down, likely to a root cellar or another storage room.

The temperature drops as I descend the stone steps, and the large wooden door at the bottom of the staircase seems to confirm my theory. Except for the key still in the lock. Frowning, I push the door open.

My lips part in surprise, but the feeling is quickly swallowed by anger. It's a room drenched in her sweet scent—Kaylin's bedroom. It can't be more than two meters square, with a tiny bed and a small set of drawers being the only sign of someone living down here.

Every other inch is covered with boxes of food. It's a root cellar *and* her room. Crossing over to her bed, I finger the threadbare blanket covering the rock-solid mattress.

All this time—all this time I thought things were good for the humans, and this is how Kaylin's been living. It's a wonder she hasn't died from a sickness contracted in this cold, dark room. I shiver.

"Jorai!" Cyra's voice is strained. There's that stab of foreboding again.

"I'm coming!" Casting one last look around Kaylin's room, I hurry back upstairs. I can't help the small breath of relief that escapes me as I leave the unnatural darkness and cramped space behind.

"Where are you?"

"Two doors down." Zeph's voice is brimming with anger.

No, no. What did they find?

Half-stumbling down the hall, I push into the room to find the three of them crowded by the dresser in a bedroom that nearly puts the palace's guest rooms to shame.

Cyra turns her wide eyes on me, tears tracing down her cheeks.

"What is it?" I can hear the confusion in my own voice. I don't know what I was expecting when I came in, but them perusing through Zianne's clothing wasn't it.

It's Zephi who reaches down and pulls out something that clinks as he lifts it.

I'm counting my breaths again. In and out. As the chain slips through his fingers. One, two. And a manacle falls from one end. In, out. Swallowing the scream of rage that's building inside. Shoving the magic down, down, down.

Raiden's words bring me to my knees.

"She's a slave."

23

Kaylin

S TARING UP INTO ORIANE'S eyes, I know that this is it. My pathetic mortal life is about to end. And I've done nothing with it, not even pay off the debt I was sold for.

"I bet you thought Jorai would be an easy catch," Oriane whispers, looking down at me. "That Ashennor would be happy he married a royal. But we've got plans for him."

Her eyes flash, and she twists on her heel, striding towards the door through which Armis and the other man have already disappeared. I deflate in relief; perhaps I might just get out of this without anyone finding out who I am.

But then, as though Oriane has heard my very thoughts, she pauses with her hand on the doorknob.

"Who are you under there, *princess?*" She spits out the final word, spinning around to glare at me.

My eyes widen.

Oriane prowls towards me, and if I didn't know better, I would think her shifted form was a cat. "I think the others would agree that knowing who you are would be ... *beneficial* to the cause."

I press my body into the chair as though I can avoid her already reaching hands.

"Yes," she says, stopping in front of me. "We need this."

Her nails scape my cheeks as her fingers slide under my mask, and she tugs. The glue pulls and tears at my skin, and I silently beg it not to give out. But with one last firm tug, it comes free.

The silence that descends over us is worse than the screaming I imagined.

"You." Oriane's voice is but a whisper, one single, wavering note of pure rage. I don't dare look up into her eyes, afraid that I will push her into the chasm she stands on the brink of.

Maybe it's the sound of my shaky breath, or the door clicking open behind her, but Oriane tips over anyway.

"You!" she screeches. The air pressure drops, the calm before the storm, and then the room is a hurricane. The air whips, tears at my skin, my clothes, and my hair.

I scrunch my stinging eyes closed and press myself as far into the chair as my bonds will allow.

In the air, under the roaring of the wind, is a wordless scream of pure rage. And I can do nothing but try to weather this true feat of power. Magic I didn't even know ran so deeply in her veins.

But Oriane is just getting started. She flies at me, and we go crashing into the hard ground, my shoulder jolting painfully.

"How dare you!" she shrieks.

Her nails find my cheek, her fist my chin, and all I know is the battery of punches, slaps, and cuts that fly my way. I do nothing. I can do nothing with the bonds cutting painfully into my wrists.

"Oriane!" That soft voice calls over the wind, and the ghost of his electricity shudders through my body. "Enough!"

I scrunch my eyes tighter.

"Stop!"

Another voice, unfamiliar, joins Midian's. And together they bring my stepsister back. The pressure of her body on mine is lifted abruptly. And I can't help but feel it was the worst thing they could possibly do. My ears ring in the emptiness that settles as her wind vanishes.

"What do you think you're doing?"

"She—" Oriane's breaths are deep and ragged. "She's no princess. She's not even fae."

The words ring around the deathly silent room.

"What?" Soft footsteps sound on the floor, and a hand roughly yanks my head up. But I keep my eyes firmly closed, trying to turn back into the stone floor as though not seeing any of them will make them vanish. "The *slave*?"

"Someone, tell me what's going on," the other voice, a woman, snaps.

"This princess is Oriane's stepsister."

"A human?" More footsteps, and a finger traces the point of the cuff on my ear. "An imposter," the woman purrs.

I crack my eyes open to find Midian and this new woman standing over me. Oriane looms behind them, chest still heaving with fury.

"But that means..." the man murmurs and I see electricity crackle across his eyes, not at all in the way it did for Jorai.

"*Yes*, Midian." Oriane's voice has gone deadly low. "She's worthless."

Midian sits back on his heels, staring down at me thoughtfully. "Well then, I assume you would like to teach her a lesson?"

The woman, with stunningly long red hair and pale skin, grins.

"Yes." My stepsister laughs, but it is not a comforting sound.

My eyes haven't been able to leave her for some time, my heart pounding in my chest as though determined to get in as many beats as it can before whatever it is she's planning happens.

In this moment, I know there is no point in appealing to her. No use in pleading. I have vastly misunderstood Oriane.

My stepsister twists on her heel and leaves the room. I stare after her, not believing my eyes. Midian and the redhead exchange a confused glance. I thought—I thought they meant to use Midian's magic on me again. The mere memory of the electricity surging through my veins is enough to make me flinch.

"I wonder what she's planning," Midian says softly, smiling down at me thoughtfully. I don't think this man has ever raised his voice, and the thought does little to comfort me.

The woman sighs. "Who cares? None of it matters to the cause." She heads towards the door without a backwards glance.

"Her body will still send a message. Where are you going, Laika?" Midian asks with a note of disappointment.

"Someone has to tell Armis and the others. We might still salvage something if the prince doesn't know what she is," the redhead throws over her shoulder and, like Oriane, she's gone.

A heavy silence falls over us. The pressure of Midian's eyes on me is nearly enough to make me buckle, but I keep my eyes firmly turned away. There is something infinitely more vulnerable in being tied up on the ground.

A soft chuckle sounds. "You learnt your lesson, did you?" he whispers, his voice closer now as he crouches in front of me. A hand grabs my chin, yanking my head around. I stare fixedly passed his ear. "But it seems it was the wrong lesson."

His thumb rubs my cheek, and I cringe. He leans in close, his breath warming my face, and cocks his head. My eyes widen. He's listening to my heart. My wild, galloping heart that might just thump its way out of my chest any second now. A slow smile spreads across his face.

"Fancy thinking you could be anything more than this. That you *were* anything more than a filthy human."

He shoves his other hand into my hair.

"Do you think Oriane might let us have some fun, Kaylin?" he sneers.

My entire body shudders, and bile rises in my throat. I tug uselessly at my bonds, but the rope just buries deeper into my skin. My eyes water at the sting. At his intentions.

He chuckles wickedly. "Saving yourself for a prince?"

"Am I interrupting something, Mid?"

I have never been so happy to hear Oriane's voice, even though it means nothing good for me. But right now, she is the evil I would prefer.

"Only a little, Ori." Midian pulls back, taking more than a few strands of my hair with him, and glances over his shoulder. His lips curl into a smile. "Oh, but that does look like fun."

"Help me get her over to the wall?"

"With pleasure."

He pulls a knife from his belt, cutting my hands free of the chair.

But before I can even process it, he's heaving me to my feet, one hand back in my hair, the other holding my hands in place behind me.

Midian throws me chest-first against the wall, his body pressing into me as he lifts one of my hands above my head. Ice-cold steel wraps around my wrist. A manacle to match the one on my ankle.

"No," I whisper. The first word that has managed to pass through my lips in an eternity. But my fear only serves to encourage him.

"Oh, yes."

He drags my other hand up, and though I try to fight back, to pull away, I'm no match for his strength. I doubt a human man would even come close to a fae male. So, what hope do I really have?

But I try it anyway. Steel clamps down on my other wrist, and Midian steps back.

"But your sister will need a clear target, won't she?" His hands grip the back of my dress and tear it straight down to barely an inch above my hips.

My body shudders, shivers, at the exposure though not a whisper of wind caresses my skin.

"Very good," Oriane says, her voice steady now.

Something slithers across the ground, following the echo of Oriane's steps as she crosses the room.

"Would you like me to count for you, Oriane?"

"Please."

There's a woosh through the air, followed by a sharp crack.

And then my back splits in two.

Through my scream I hear Midian's voice say, "One."

My body is quaking now, the chains keeping my arms raised above my head clanking in time with each shiver. Warmth trickles down my skin.

Then comes another crack, the whip slashing into the muscle by my shoulder.

This time, Midian has to raise his voice to be heard over the screams that tear at my throat. He does it for the benefit of my human ears.

"Two."

Swoosh. Crack. Scream.

"Three."

Swoosh. Crack. Scream.

"Four."

By five, I haven't stopped screaming. My hands have twisted in the shackles to grip the chains. To keep me upright, to keep me awake.

"Six."

My dress is heavy. Warm. Wet.

I don't hear seven.

24

Jorai

"**T**HEY'LL KILL HER IF they find out who she is." I hardly recognise my own voice. But there it is. The truth. I've killed Kaylin simply by dancing with her.

"We're not going to let that happen," Cyra says, kneeling down to grab my hands. "We'll find her."

But it's Raiden that I look to. "Where do we go from here?" I press.

Rage shines in his eyes, but it's not directed at me. His knuckles have gone white as he grips the chain in his hand. "I assume your citizens have to register purchases of land with the Crown?"

I cock my head. "Yes."

"Then we need to look at all land registered to Zianne, Oriane, Faina, and anyone associated with them. She won't be in any of their homes."

With a plan in mind, I'm able to focus. Calm myself. "Let's go."

"There's nothing here!" I throw the pile of parchment I've been rifling through to the record room's floor. Zephi glances up from his own stack of papers.

"There must be something."

I run a hand through my hair, shoving at the panic threatening to rise again. I need to keep a clear head, or I won't be of any help. Not to Kaylin, not to anyone.

"Is there anyone else who might be involved?" Raiden asks, pushing away his pile. Cyra simply adds his to her own. "Where's Kaylin's father?" he adds almost as an afterthought.

A fire ignites in Cyra's eyes. "I don't know, but I'm sure he knows exactly what's happened to Kaylin in that house. If he knows what's good for him, he'll never show his face here again. Though, I suspect that was his plan."

I find myself nodding. I'd like to ask him a few questions myself, but I can't think about that now.

"Zianne and Oriane have friends in the court, but we've checked all their close contacts," I say. "And they don't have any lovers—" But Zianne did. She had a husband once.

"Jory? What is it?"

My heart gives a distracted pang. Cyra and Kaylin are the only people to ever call me Jory. It was Kaylin who started it, the very day we met.

"What if it's in Lael's name?" I say slowly.

Cyra's brow crinkles. "Zianne's husband? But he died decades ago."

"Exactly."

She jumps to her feet. "We need to be quick. I don't know how long Eran will let us go on." My aunt disappears down one of the corridors of shelves brimming with parchments.

I can feel Raiden's eyes on me.

"I understand if you can't come with us the rest of the way," I say, catching his eye.

He has bigger things to worry about, after all. And who knows what my father will do if he finds out Frigarth helped me? Raiden still has time to get to the festival and ensure he's seen where I am not.

Understanding lights in his blue eyes, darker than mine and yet they feel like a brother's.

"I will not turn away now."

"Thank you."

"You'll need all the help you can get if you're to succeed. These people are dedicated."

I grimace. How could I have been so foolish not to take their threats seriously? Not to insist my father do something *real* to stop them.

"It is done, Jorai," Raiden says. And Zephi glances up, looking between us. "What matters is what you do now."

My captain nods his approval.

"I can't make any promises for my father," I say, "but *I* won't let this continue."

"I've found it!" Cyra's voice rings out, even as she runs back to our group, hair bouncing in time with her footfalls.

She slaps a blueprint down on the table. "They're under-ground."

Raiden is on his feet in an instant, towering over Cyra as he studies the map.

The structure is two levels—underground as Cyra said—with several winding corridors and rooms. But it seems clear to me where Kaylin will be. In the deepest room, furthest from the light, and with the oldest, foulest air. Because they'd planned for a fae princess, and such a place would have been torture in and of itself.

I can't tear myself away from the outline of that room. As though by staring at it hard enough I might see her, and she might know that I'm coming.

"I can make this work. But we'll need a couple more guards," Raiden says, his fingers tracing the lines of the blueprint. "She'll be in here." His finger taps on the room I've been staring at.

"I'll get the men," Zephi adds, gripping my shoulder before hurrying from the room.

"Can you distract my father?" I don't glance up, but my aunt knows I'm speaking to her.

She snorts. "Screw Eran. I'm coming with you."

"Cyra." I tear my gaze away, up to her fierce face. The tears stopped long ago, and now in their place is a raging fury, a steady determination that I wouldn't dare try to smother. "You'll need a weapon."

She grins without humour, waving her hand. "I'm a princess. I'm never unarmed."

Raiden gives her an approving smile. "I wouldn't expect anything less from you, Cyra." It's an innocent enough comment, but I wonder just how much he knows about her past. Perhaps we're not the only ones who did our research before his visit.

"So, what's the plan?" I ask.

Raiden's smile fades. "There's only one entrance, and getting in will be the hardest part." He leans in. "This is what we'll do."

25

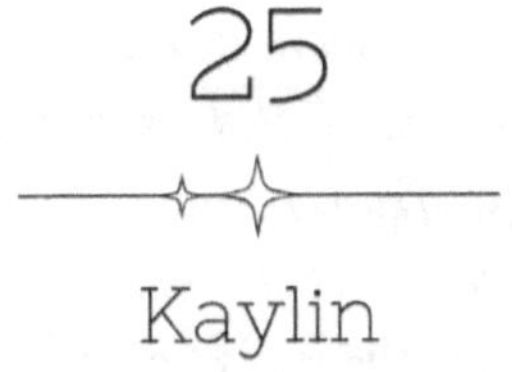

Kaylin

"*P*APA!" I RACE AFTER *my father, latching onto his shirt. It hangs nearly to his knees and sits loosely off his frame.*

He pushes me away, ripping his shirt from my fingers. He stares down at me with dark, empty eyes, and I wish he'd smile once more for me, like he used too before mum died. He shakes his head, his grimy hair, blonde like mine, catching the light.

"You're to stay here, Kaylin." His words are slurred. He's sick again. He always speaks funny when he's sick. He needs a doctor. Why won't he see a doctor? The tang of his medicine clings to him, but it doesn't work. It never has.

"You have a debt to pay off now, Kaylin." Papa's boss takes my hand, a kind smile on her face, but there's something about her silver eyes that make me uneasy.

"Because of Papa's medicine?"

She laughs. "Yes, because of his medicine."

My father's eyes darken, but he doesn't say anything.

"Goodbye, Maaz." Zianne pulls me back inside the house before I get the chance to say anything, and Papa doesn't follow. I watch as he turns to leave.

Zianne crouches beside me. "You're to call me Stepmother from now on, Kaylin."

"But Papa will be back soon, won't he?"

Her lips curl into a grin, but she says nothing.

Zianne pulls a knife from inside her dress. My eyes widen, and I try to pull away, but she holds me firm. She presses the blade to the skin on the inside of my arm, sending drops running down my bicep.

With a cry, I finally yank my arm free, but she smiles, collecting a drop of the liquid with her finger. "That's all I need."

Zianne walks deeper into the house, but instead of following, I watch my father's figure disappearing down the road in an awkward shuffle. I glance behind me to see where Zianne is, but I can't see her.

Smiling, I pull up my hem and run after my father.

"Come here."

I've made it barely three steps when her voice sounds from within the house. My body freezes. A tingle goes through me, rakes its finger down my spine, and my feet turn and lead the way unbidden.

And though I scream, there is no stopping this body that is no longer mine.

A soft breeze caresses my face, and I crack my eyes open in the cold darkness. I gulp the fresh air down greedily, but it fades all too quickly, leaving me with the stale air now tainted with the tang of my own blood and sweat.

I'm still by the wall, for I can see it through the gloom. My hands are still chained, though the rebels have let my body slump to the ground.

There must be some kind of lever or wheel to tighten and loosen the restraints. A new manacle has been placed over the scars of my right ankle, connecting to my left. But the stillness of the room tells me I'm mercifully alone.

My back is a raging fire, and I don't dare shift even a millimetre to test my bonds.

"You idiot," I whisper in the darkness, a broken croak. I don't recognise the voice that leaves me.

I screw up my fists. If I hadn't agreed to go to the festival again, none of this would have happened. The 'princess' would have become a distant memory, and I would have been safe. Waiting for a father that never really planned to come back.

But still safe. It's the memory of the festival that I find myself clinging to, though. Of Jorai's hands at my waist, of the dancing. Of us.

The one thing I can look back on in my life from the last ten years with joy.

I should have told him who I was. So that I could have one memory from the festival that was *real*. One memory that was *truly* us.

A shiver wracks through my body, and I moan as the skin and blood on my back cracks and shifts.

Jorai. He was everything I remembered him to be. He was kind and sweet and funny and he *looked* at me even just for a moment. And maybe that matters.

I sniff, my eyes watering. Maybe no one's going to come for me. Maybe I will die down here, but maybe I did matter for a moment. I mattered to Cyra enough that she remembered me all these years. Jorai cared for me for those two infinite days …. And it was only because I stood up to Zianne.

Why should I regret the festival? Why should I wish I never went? For once, for *once* in my worthless, mortal life I was truly living.

And even though I'm lying on a cold, stone floor drenched in my own blood, I smile.

I smile through the tears leaking from my heavy eyes. In taking my life, Oriane helped me find it.

26

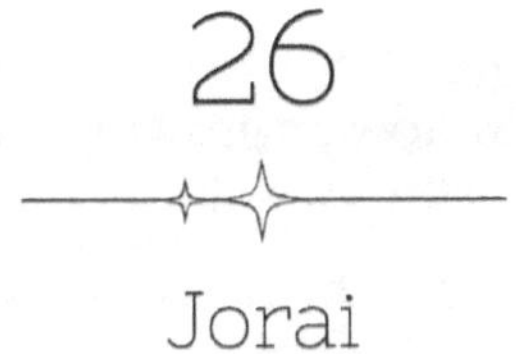

Jorai

IT'S NEARLY DUSK WHEN we finally set out to find Kaylin. The rebels have had her for nearly twenty-four hours now. My stomach churns at the very thought. It would have been better to wait until night settled before our attack, but there's not a second to lose.

We leave the palace on foot under the guise of showing Raiden more of the city on our way to the festival. Fine cloaks hide our tactical clothing and weapons—a dead give-away of our real destination. It was Raiden's idea, to stop word getting out to the rebels that an attack force was on its way.

Two guards accompany us, while another two are making their own way to the rebels' hiding place alone. I force my feet to stop, my fingers to point at interesting buildings and fountains and statues, meaningless words passing through my lips. Then we hurry on.

"Slower, Jor," Zephi warns.

I growl in frustration, dropping back from a near jog.

"A little further," Raiden murmurs, scanning the roads, the buildings, without turning his head. His blades are on his back, but that's not unusual for him.

"Oh, and this one!" Cyra gasps, yanking on mine and Raiden's arms to bring us to a stop in front of a small, cream building with golden flowers growing from the front face. "This is one of my favourites," she gushes, bouncing on her toes. But her eyes betray the falseness of the enjoyment in her voice. The rage that still simmers underneath.

"It's beautiful, my lady," Raiden says. "I've not seen so many elansi's growing in one place."

"I know a place with even more!" And she finally turns us towards Kaylin.

Her hand doesn't loosen on my mine, but she gives it a gentle squeeze and leads the way.

The buildings begin to thin, their lands spreading out around them. The Iden Mountains loom in the distance, north of the city we're leaving behind.

We can no longer hide ourselves in sightseeing, so we spread out, creeping from hiding place to hiding place. The longer we can go without being spotted, the better chance we have of getting to Kaylin.

A small, stone building comes into view and by unsaid agreement, we all pause. There is no sign of any fae or human. The garden around it has been left to grow wild, the vines crawling wildly up the stone walls and onto the roof. Clearly a human design, I wonder what Lael had planned for this place.

To anyone else it would look abandoned. But I'm sure this is it. I can't let myself think of the possibility that we could be wrong again.

I glance at Raiden and nod.

Without a word, Raiden shifts. When he'd mentioned his animal form in the palace, I could hardly believe our luck. Mine and Zephi's are too large to go unnoticed, and Cyra's form is well-known. But Raiden, who now sits before us as a simple rook, will go unnoticed by any fae rebel on the lookout for an attack.

He spreads his black wings and jumps into the air, flying out over the building in a seemingly lazy arc.

Kaylin

The door opens behind me with a long creak before slamming. I listen intently, keeping my eyes closed. If they think I'm still unconscious, maybe they'll leave me alone. Maybe they'll say something to give away where I am.

I chide myself. It doesn't matter where I am.

I'm not fool enough to think I can get myself out of here in this condition and with at least three adult fae down here with me.

Low murmurs sound from the corner, I can't make out their words, but instantly I can tell something is wrong. Their tones are rushed, urgent. Something's happening.

"We should do it now." The edge to Midian's words, that he surely meant for me to hear, is enough to tell me everything, and my blood runs cold. I barely keep from flinching and giving myself away.

So, this is it. I clench my fists, the movement sending pain through my body.

I might have no hope of leaving, but I won't go down easy. I'll make the memory of the human slave they killed for simply daring to live burn brightly in their minds.

Hundreds of years from now, they'll still remember me.

"Not yet," Oriane hisses. "He needs to be here."

He. My mind races. There are still two men missing from Zianne's dinner; Armis and the man who hit me. I instantly dismiss the idea of the second man. He was cruel, but he didn't have the same presence as Armis. Is he their leader? Perhaps Oriane didn't need permission to whip me, but she needs it to kill me?

"Put her in the chair," Oriane orders.

"Careful, Ori, he might bite," Laika purrs, her voice floating through the air. "Midian doesn't like being told what to do."

Three. They're all back. And once Armis arrives, that'll be it. My lifespan has dropped from potentially hours down to minutes.

I take one deep, steadying breath.

"Listening in, are we?"

I nearly jump out of my skin at the deep growl that sounds above me and gasp as pain shoots through my body. Armis is already here.

The massive fae grabs my arm, dragging me upright, and agony rages through me. My head swirls and the room sways. When it becomes clear my legs won't support my body, Armis drags me across the room. Through blurry vision I see the figures of Oriane, Laika, and Midian standing in a cluster by the door.

Midian's eyes gleam as they fall on me, and the hand on the hilt of his sword twitches, electricity shining. Laika barely spares me a glance as Armis throws me down on the chair.

I bite down on the scream brewing in my throat as my body sways.

Oriane tuts, prowling over to us.

"Trying to be brave, Kaylin?" She stops in front of me, and instead of staring down at her feet, I slowly raise my eyes to meet hers. No hope, only living.

Anger flares in her gaze, but I refuse to be cowed anymore. I might have lived as a slave, but I won't die one.

She grabs the chain linking my hands together and yanks my arms up and back. This time I can't hold back the scream as my entire back lights on fire. Warmth flows down my skin even as she clips my chains to the chair behind me.

"You may have finally found your courage, but it doesn't matter. Mother says he's coming for you. And he's going to watch you die," she whispers in my ear.

My heart stutters at her declaration. Jorai is coming for me?

"Leave him alone!" I croak, my voice tearing at my ruined vocal cords.

The fae chuckle, their laughter echoing in the small room.

Armis, too, laughs as he looks down on me, but I see the ripple of warning in his muscles, and it gives me a moment to brace for the impact of the fist that swiftly comes down on my face.

Pain rockets through me, and for several seconds I can't see or hear anything as the blow reverberates around my broken body. All I can do is force one deep breath through my lungs after another, as the pain slowly recedes and I taste blood in my mouth, feel it pouring from my lip.

When I'm finally able to blink away the tears and focus my mind on the present, Armis is gone. Only Oriane and Midian remain. And the twisted smiles on their faces nearly breaks me.

What are they going to do to Jorai?

27

Jorai

I HOLD UP THREE fingers, locking eyes with the huge wolf on the other side of the entranceway. Zephi shifted as soon as we were close enough for him to get a scent in this form. His fur is thick and white, and his back reaches nearly to my waist. His eyes are still his even as a wolf, a dark brown.

He blinks his understanding, and I glance at Raiden, who is now back in his fae form, Cyra, and then the four guards. They all nod, and I slowly lower my fingers in a silent countdown. At zero, Zephi dives through the entranceway and I'm right behind him, my magic crackling in the air, ready to be summoned in an instant.

The building is barely five meters long and even less in width. Except for an old moss-covered table in the far corner, it's empty of any furnishings. And in the centre, charging towards us, are the two armed fae males Raiden reported.

With a howl, Zephi jumps forwards, barrelling into one of the men and sending him sprawling on the ground with a pained grunt.

I duck a strike from the other man and thrust my hand out, sending a powerful gust of wind slamming into his chest.

"Let's go!" I shout, striding around the room in search of the trapdoor that leads underground.

Two of the guards step forwards to deal with the fae males, both in the process of rising to their feet.

"Zeph!" I call.

Zephi abandons the rebel with a reluctant growl, but I'll need him for whatever we find below. And though I don't want to admit it, I might need him to help me with *myself*. My grip on my magic is still on a knife's edge, singing for me to release it, to let it run rampant.

But I can't afford to lose control. Especially not with Kaylin, a mortal, down there.

"Here!" Cyra shouts, pointing to a spot on the floor.

I jog over, leaves crunching under my feet. If you didn't know what to look for, you wouldn't know it was there.

The door, no wider than my shoulders, is built from the same stone as the flooring to help disguise it. But the stones are cleaner, lacking the dirt, vines, and moss of the rest of the floor. And there is a slightly larger gap between the stones that mark the edge. I dig my fingers into them, looking for purchase.

"Allow me, Your Highness." Taavi steps forwards, sheathing his blade.

I fight with myself for a moment, but if there's any-one down there, we'll need Taavi and the remaining guard, Holden, to keep them busy while the rest of us move on. I nod, stepping back.

Once in position, he looks at me. "Ready?"

My grip tightens on my sword. "Ready."

He heaves the door up and open, then drops down into the darkness.

A low grunt echoes up, followed by the ring of steel on steel. Zephi leaps after him, but I don't get down until the other guard has also pushed his way through. When I finally land in the damp shadows, a woman lies unconscious on the ground. Taavi stands over her, a bruise already forming on his cheekbone.

"I know her," I whisper, studying the woman's dark-skinned face. "I've seen her in the markets."

"Tie her up," Raiden says as he lands beside Holden, gesturing to the man.

"Follow when you're done," I add.

"Yes, Your Highness."

I peer down the hallway, summoning an image of the blueprints in my mind.

We were forced to leave them behind—there'd be no time to stop and spread them out on the floor. It may be dark enough for a human to be blind down here, but I can see several meters ahead.

"It's eerie down here," Cyra says, a shudder going through her body. "We need to get her out."

We've been down here not five minutes and already the darkness and stale air rankles us. And they planned to keep a fae princess down here. They *are* keeping one.

My magic flares and the air crackles, but I shove it back and break into a run down the hallway. I'd better find Kaylin healthy and whole. Because I'm beginning to wonder if Zephi will be enough to stop me.

At the third junction a fae man leaps out from my right, and the glint of a dagger is all the warning I have before Zephi barrels me aside. His powerful jaws lock on the man's wrist, and his scream bounces off the stone wall, stabbing into my ears. Taavi has pushed forward, drawing on the damp air and sending a stream of water into the man's face.

"Go, go!" he shouts, forcing the male backwards with his magic.

"Zeph!" I yell over my shoulder as I continue down the hall, Raiden and Cyra close behind.

My captain will be frustrated with abandoning his prey again, but we have to stick to the plan. We're already out of soldiers to keep the rebels busy, and we've not even reached the second level.

I may have underestimated just how many there are. Again. But just maybe, they've done the same with us.

A snarl of frustration escapes my lips, sounding exactly like my shifted form. But I can't afford to change into the big cat, not when my magic offers a greater advantage. A growl of anger, or perhaps sympathetic agreement, sounds from Zephi, who easily trots beside me.

His nose is leading the way now, making sure we're not wrong in our guess of where they're keeping Kaylin.

But I would trade it all, all my magic and my shifted form, just to have the power to tell her I'm coming. That she'll be safe before the night's over. That I won't ever leave her.

Zephi stops, sniffing the air.

"The stairs should be around here," Raiden murmurs.

"They are," Cyra says, pushing forwards. "Down that hall." She turns to me, her eyes heavy as she holds mine. "I'll distract the guard. Get her out, Jory."

Before I can stop her, my aunt shoots down the hall, gripping a long dagger tightly in her hand.

"Cyra!" I hiss, but she's gone.

"We need to get there before someone else comes up," Raiden warns.

I swallow. "Right."

"I'll go first," the ambassador says, pushing forwards.

I should stop him, stop an incident forming between our countries, but Raiden himself suggested this plan. And I'll do almost anything to get Kaylin out.

It's time to put the ambassador's skill to the test.

I nod, in agreement.

Within a couple meters, a hole in the floor looms out of the darkness, revealing stone stairs leading downwards. Cyra is nowhere to be seen, but neither is the guard. Raiden descends first, a sword gripped in each hand. Zephi follows, his paws padding silently on the stone. I bring up the rear, feeling my magic crackle with anticipation.

Raiden pauses on the bottom step before entering the hall below.

"The ambassador?" a deep voice growls, carrying up the stairs. It sparks a familiarity in me, but I can't quite place the voice.

"Frigarth has made its opinion clear."

"Indeed," the man says, a deep laugh shining through his voice. "We didn't expect to teach three lessons tonight."

Zephi emerges behind Raiden, and he loosens a low growl.

"Captain," the man says as though greeting an old acquaintance for lunch.

It's not until I reach the last step that the man comes completely into view.

"Armis. I should have known Faina was lying."

The court male's face darkens. "You have my sister?"

What was Faina supposed to be doing now that he hadn't noticed her absence? I shake the thought from my head, rage chasing it away.

"You have my—Kaylin."

Armis smiles, the gesture not quite reaching his eyes, as he slowly spins the spear in his grip.

"What's left of her."

What's left of her. I've launched myself at him before I know what I'm doing. A wordless roar is echoing off the walls. Me.

I slam my blade down into the shaft of his spear again and again, heedless of all else. Electricity crackles along my skin, and blood spurts in my mouth as my canines elongate before I can rein the shift in. Armis doesn't yield a step, and his spear is strong, forged with the lightest of metals. My blade does little more than nick it.

Growling, I change direction at the last moment, swiping my sword around and under as he prepares to receive another blow from above. But Armis is a skilled fighter, and he manages to stop my blade before it buries more than a centimetre into his abdomen.

He shoves me back, my blade ringing along the length of his spear. But I'm diving forwards again, hearing nothing but those words echoing in my ears and the fear, the absolutely terrifying thought that I might be too late.

Armis nimbly steps aside, deftly spinning his spear to bring the end up and slamming into my jaw. My head snaps to the side, but I'm upon him again, punching his face with my sword's hilt.

The big man stumbles back, but a hand clamps down on my shoulder before I can follow.

"Jorai, leave him to me. Go find her."

I can barely hear Raiden's voice over the heaving of my own breaths, but he squeezes my shoulder again. I stumble back, reining in my magic and firmly stamping it down, letting Raiden take the lead. He advances on Armis, who flashes him a wicked grin through bloodied lips, but I don't stop to watch.

I bolt down the hall, with Zephi bounding on my heels. The air grows even thicker, and I wrinkle my nose at the smell. I never knew air to be this stale or still. I doubt this place has ever had a fresh gust of wind.

We turn left, right, left again and finally the door comes into view. I fight the urge to slow down, the fear that makes me wonder what it is I'm going to find.

Armis's words echo in my mind. *What's left of her.*

Exchanging a glance with Zephi, I push into the room.

28

Jorai

IT's THE SMELL THAT hits me first. The iron tang of human blood. And lots of it. I stumble to a stop in the doorway, overcome by the scent and the sight of what lies before me.

Kaylin is sprawled in a wooden chair in the centre of the room, only upright because of the chains holding her wrists and ankles together. She's still in the dress she wore last night, except it's in ruins. The white, golden, and silver feathers are now a deep red, the fabric torn and barely covering her. A purple bruise has blossomed on her cheek, and blood has spilled from the split in her lower lip. Where once she looked pale, now she looks like a corpse. The air begins to crackle.

Perhaps roused by my magic, Kaylin's eyes open and scan the room, widening as they land on me. Her lips part, but not a whisper passes through them. She blinks hard as though not trusting her eyes.

The surprise in them is like a knife to my heart. Had she thought I wouldn't come? Even after knowing who she is?

"Finally! We were beginning to wonder whether you'd make it before your darling *princess* expired."

My skin crawls at the familiar voice, and it takes more than a supreme effort of will to tear my gaze from Kaylin. Oriane stands against the wall behind her, but as I watch, she pushes off, prowling across the room.

"I wondered if you knew what she was? You certainly do now, with the stench of her on the air."

Stopping directly behind Kaylin, she draws a blade.

"Don't you touch her!" Lightning dances on my fingers. It extinguishes instantly. But not at my command.

Zephi growls a low warning, and Midian steps out from behind the door. I didn't even check for others.

"Careful, Your Highness," he says, a cheerless smile curving his lips, "you wouldn't want to hurt her, now would you?"

"Midian?"

I look between Oriane and Midian. Just how much of my father's court and the respected fae are a part of the rebels? With Armis and Faina ...

"What is this?" I hiss between gritted teeth.

Oriane slowly lowers her knife, placing it against the skin of Kaylin's neck. "This is us finally being heard. And with Midian here to snuff your powers, you have no choice but to listen."

I don't react, internalising the realisation that my lifelong bluff is playing off in this moment. They think my lightning is my worst power, perhaps my only one, and that gives me a chance.

Midian carefully crosses the room, coming to a stop beside Kaylin.

I don't miss the way her heartbeat quickens as he looks down at her, though not a flicker of her fear shows on her face.

"All right," I say, biting back the rage threatening to erupt. I need to be careful. I need an opportunity. "I'm listening."

Zephi stays beside me, his eyes locked on Midian. But there's nothing he can do while Midian wields his electrical magic. He could kill with a single hit.

But Midian hasn't had the same level of training I have. As a weather wielder, I have learned to know my ability inside out and to levels that others may never reach with their own powers.

And Midian has never cared for the finer points of lightning. Slowly, I twist the magic deep inside me, forcing it to do the opposite of what it wants. I begin to lower the charge in the air, stifling Midian's magic by the tiniest increments.

Oriane chuckles darkly. "Things are so much worse than we feared. When we saw you dancing with a fae, we thought there was still hope. But then we saw what she was, and clearly you don't *care*."

The blade in her hand wobbles.

"Careful, Oriane. You hurt her anymore, and you've lost my attention."

"Oh, no," she says, a wicked grin lighting her face. "I'm not going to hurt her. I'm going to kill her. And then you're going to put the humans back in their place where they belong."

I swallow heavily, forcing my magic back as it flares. I can't do anything while the knife is at Kaylin's throat, while Midian remains a threat to Zephi.

"You know we can't do that," I growl through clenched teeth. It's a huge effort not to shift, not to unleash my magic and tear this room apart. I keep dialling down the charge. "It would break the alliance with Frigarth."

"I know." Oriane lowers her face to be level with Kaylin's, and a bead of blood forms around the blade. "Give me your word, and I'll make it quick."

Kaylin's eyes are locked on mine, agony in her eyes. But something else is there, too. Determination. She flicks her eyes towards Midian, then sideways towards where Oriane's face is just behind her. I keep my expression blank, but my mind is racing. What is she trying to say?

Midian frowns. Twitches his fingers. I'm running out of time. He suspects what I'm doing. And I'm no closer to getting Kaylin free.

"It's not my decision," I say, trying to buy time. Trying to lower the charge and increase the humidity.

Oriane sighs, but then several things happen at once. Kaylin whips her head back, slamming into her stepsister's face. Oriane stumbles back and the blade nicks the side of Kaylin's neck.

Midian yells, kicking the chair out from under Kaylin, who goes slamming into the floor. And I see her back. *Her back.* Suddenly, all the blood makes sense. The ruined dress. The agony in her eyes. Her flesh is ravaged.

Someone is roaring, someone is yelling, and it's me and all I can see is red and my lightning and rain and wind bursting through the room, whipping at Midian and Oriane, tearing at their clothes and skin. Burning them, sending electricity through their bodies.

But not Kaylin, and not Zephi. No, for once I am in control. My emotions, my rage granting me power as I throw magic from my body as I have hardly dared to do before.

Midian attempts to rally, throwing out his hands to form a protective shield from the lighting around him and Oriane. He tries to pull it from my grip, but I keep it firmly in my grasp. My magic runs deeper, my family older and drenched in more power than his could ever gain in a hundred generations.

Zephi lets loose a long howl, then leaps forwards, his fur standing on end from the charge in the room. His powerful jaws close on Midian's arm, and the weak shield drops.

But I don't shoot my lightning at them. I want them to rot for their crimes. Instead, I send a great rush of wind and water into Oriane, flinging her backwards into the wall where she slumps unconscious. I leave Midian to Zephi.

·)🌒🌒🌑🌘🌘(·

Kaylin

"Kaylin? Open your eyes for me, love. Please."

His voice sounds miles away, echoing down a long tunnel. He can't be here. I must have dreamed Jorai came, dreamed the way his face paled at the sight of me. The anger there.

"Kaylin. Please." Jorai's voice is a broken sob. My mind struggles to rise from the pain and exhaustion pulling me down, but his is a call I could never ignore. His hand is on my face, gently brushing my hair back. I feel his fingers caress my ears with the movement.

"That's it. Come on, love."

"Jory?" I don't recognise the croak that escapes my lips. My voice is just as ruined as my body.

"Yes," he gasps. "Yes! Open your eyes for me. Come on."

It's a great effort to force them to open, the weight of every ache weighing down on my lids. But they do, and when they finally clear, Jorai is the first thing that I see.

His face is nearly as pale as mine must be, but the smile he gives me is the widest I've ever seen. My mind whirls. He was angry, wasn't he?

"Hello," he whispers.

"I'm sorry," I murmur, my lips stiff with blood.

"What for?" he says, his thumb caressing my cheek.

I'm still on the ground, my arms and legs still chained, but the tension in them has lessened. Jorai looks too afraid to touch me anywhere but my face, too afraid to move me.

"For everything. For all of this." A tear leaks from the corner of my eye.

"No, I'm sorry," he says, his eyes not leaving mine. "I should have listened when they told me there were still humans in slavery."

Slavery. I close my eyes. He knows.

"Kaylin—"

"I found it!" a familiar voice calls from behind me.

I snap my eyes open as Captain Zephi appears beside Jorai, his black hair wild and a key in his hand.

"My lady," he says gently, looking down on me.

I frown, but Jorai has grabbed the key and shifts behind me, revealing the room.

Oriane and Midian lie unconscious in the corner opposite me, piled roughly together, their limbs bound.

"Support her arms for me, Zeph."

The captain ducks behind me as well.

"We'll move you as little as we can until it's time to go, Kaylin."

"OK," I croak, trying to stop my body from tensing in anticipation.

Gentle, warm hands close just above the manacles and I can't stop my body from flinching at the touch. I hiss.

"I'm sorry," Zephi says softly.

A lock clicks, and the manacle around my left wrist drops free. The captain carefully pulls it away. Just as Jorai inserts the key into the other manacle, the door to the room bursts open. Cyra runs in, closely followed by a large fae man with white hair.

"Oh, Kaylin!" she shouts, dropping to her knees in front of me. Her hair is a mess, the blonde curls loose around her face and smeared with dirt and blood. "I'm sorry, darling. I'm sorry I didn't know—I didn't find you sooner," she gushes.

"It's fine." I wince as the other manacle falls free.

Cyra frowns, then carefully leans over to look at my back.

"Who did this?" I have never heard my godmother's voice so low and deadly.

The eyes of the man behind her snap to her, and he strides forwards. But he doesn't stop to gawk at what's left of my back; instead, he places a steadying hand on her shoulder. There's nothing romantic in the touch, nothing sensual, but the tension leaks from her body and Cyra pulls back, her hands cupping my face.

"It'll be alright, the healers will make quick work of it," she assures me, voice tender.

"Let's get your legs free, Kaylin," Jorai says.

I can't bring myself to tell him that only one of them will come free. That the other is a decade old. But I don't have to tell him, as a change in the atmosphere a moment later reveals he's seen my scars, the cloths shoved under the old manacle in an attempt to lessen the rubbing.

Cyra's eyes flick to my ankles but she says nothing, simply stroking my face.

"Let's get you out of here, darling," she murmurs, pressing a soft kiss to my forehead.

The white-haired fae seems to exchange a long look with Jorai and Captain Zephi. My back. They don't know how to move me.

"Give me your cloak, Raiden," Jory says, his voice rough.

The fae man with Cyra unclips his cloak and hands it to Jorai. "It won't be enough to hold her."

"No," Jorai says. "But it will help."

He comes around in front of me, and Cyra makes room for him.

"I'm going to drape this over your back, Kaylin. But I'll have to carry you to get you out of here. We can't wait for the healers to come."

I nod, biting back a sob. I don't want to move. I don't want anyone to even touch me.

"Zeph, help me turn her."

I can't hold back the tears from my eyes as they get into position. The mere thought of moving is agony.

"We'll be quick, love," Jorai whispers.

I'm not ashamed of the whimper that leaves me. Or the scream that tears my throat as they carefully lift and turn my body.

But then I'm in Jorai's arms, his scent wrapping around me even as oblivion finally closes my eyes.

It's not such a bad place to die.

29

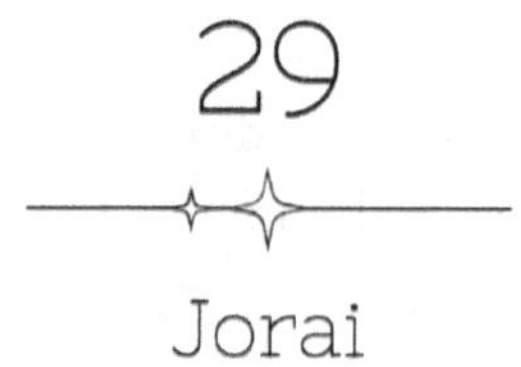

Jorai

"It seems you managed to bring into custody a large portion of the rebels and all on your own?" my father grumbles into the silence that has settled over our group at the end of my recount of all that happened.

I don't correct him, don't implicate the soldiers that came with us, though I'm sure he has his suspicions who they were.

"Furthermore," he says after a long moment, "two were caught in the attempt of rescuing Faina. They remain in custody."

"And Zianne?" I ask. There's no way she wasn't involved with the rebels, but even if she wasn't, she's done more than enough to Kaylin to warrant an arrest.

"The guards found her attending the festival," my father says, his brow crinkling. "She's in the dungeon, too. She maintains her innocence."

I take a deep breath as my magic stirs. What was she doing at the festival? Had she attended as a spy for the rebels?

"Clearly a lie." I'm impressed with how normal my voice sounds. "Interrogations will need to start immediately if we're to have any chance of catching more of them."

My father's brow drops again, but he says nothing of my audacity.

"Yes. Captain," he says, turning to Zephi, "you will be in charge of everything related to the rebels."

"Yes, Your Majesty," he replies with a bow.

Coming to see my father could have gone either way for us, particularly for Zephi and Raiden. Especially since I made him wait until the healers had finished with Kaylin and I knew she would be OK. It was nearly noon when we all finally came to see him. And I'm itching to get back to her.

"And the girl?" my father asks, his thoughts clearly following mine. His eyes drift over our group; over me, Cyra (whose face has hardened defensively at the mention of her goddaughter), Zephi, and finally landing on Raiden.

The ambassador has said little, but he asked me not to conceal his role in the rescue as I have with Taavi and the others.

"She'll stay here with me," I say. "If she wants to." If she'll have me. But if she won't, she's still more than welcome to stay.

I would see her safe and happy for the remainder of her days even if they're not with me. But I can't deny that my time with her, in recent days and in years past, have been the happiest of my life. I never realised just how empty the time in between was.

His blue eyes narrow, landing on the shoe that's still ridiculously tucked into my belt, and he sits back in his chair with a long sigh.

"Quite an advantageous marriage," Raiden says in a calm voice. "It would certainly solidify the promise of equality and Ashennor's friendship with Frigarth. King Turin and Queen Laurel would approve."

The king says nothing, and I can see his mind racing. He hates that we've put him in this position. That *I* have. And yet he can't deny how good it would look if Kaylin were to live here, whether with me or with Cyra as her godmother.

"Very well."

"Good." I rise, unwilling to waste more time where I'm not at Kaylin's side.

"Jorai," my father says, his back to me now as he looks out over the garden. There's a long pause as though he's collecting his thoughts or even himself. "I ... Well done."

"Thank you, Father." I leave the room with a smile on my face, closely followed by my friends. I've no doubt this will take my father time to adjust to, but his willingness is enough for me.

The sun is shining brightly today, hitting the starlight at just the right angle. The palace looks stunning. I'm weightless as we walk.

"I will drop by to see you later, Jorai. I'm needed in the dungeon," Zephi's low voice says from behind me.

"Thank you, Zeph."

With a nod, he breaks away from our group.

Cyra grabs my arm, her eyes sparkling. "I need to change and wash up. I'll meet you there?"

I nod, squeezing her hand before she hurries off. None of us have slept since the night before Kaylin was taken. The exhaustion hangs over us like a thick cloud and yet I don't think any of us are ready to sleep either.

I stop in my tracks abruptly. There's one thing I had forgotten to say in all the chaos of getting Kaylin back here and healed.

I turn to Raiden, finding his puzzled blue eyes already on me.

"Raiden, I—"

"I know," Raiden says, cutting me off. "We'll talk later. Go be with her when she wakes up."

I gape at him, then smile. "Frigarth is lucky to have you, Ambassador."

"Oh, they know." He shoots me a grin. "Don't forget to give her that shoe back."

I laugh, but I have something far better than a shoe for her.

Raiden twists on his heel and strides away.

Shaking my head, I break into a sprint, heading for Kaylin's room.

30

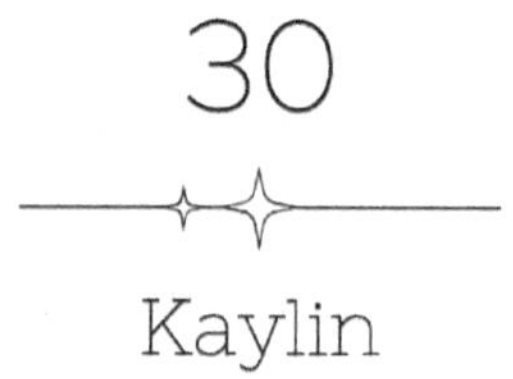

Kaylin

WAKING UP IS EXHAUSTING. I emerge slowly from a deep but blessedly empty sleep, unsure if I want to throw off the darkness's reaching arms. I don't want to wake and find myself in that prison. To find that Jorai's rescue was nothing more than a dream.

I told myself I would be strong, but I couldn't face another day in there. But a ray of warmth across my face and body has me pausing, and the soft caress of a breeze across my skin makes me turn eagerly towards consciousness.

Blinking my eyes open, I find myself looking up at a ceiling of starlight with bright beams of sunshine streaking across it.

"Kaylin?"

I gasp as Jorai leans over me.

It was *real.*

"How are you feeling, love?" he says, taking my hand in his.

"I—" I blink. I'm tired, I'm exhausted beyond anything I've felt in a long time, and yet my body doesn't hurt. I'm lying on my ruined back, but there's no pain.

My wrists are no longer sore or bound, and my lip doesn't feel swollen.

And Jorai is holding my hand.

"Am I dead?" I whisper.

"No," he chuckles, brushing a strand of hair back from my face. "No, love."

I frown, tearing my eyes from him to look around. I'm in the palace, that much is clear from the starlight around me. It's an outer room with no walls in order to let the sunlight in. But the fae have allowed me a rare gift of privacy, stringing curtains up around the borders of the room. The bed I'm in is more than double the size of my cot back home. A silk sheet covers my body.

"It's OK," Jorai assures me, perhaps seeing the confusion on my face. "You're safe here. You're all right."

"I don't feel anything?" I say, catching his gaze. My mind is a confusion of images. I remember Jorai, Cyra, the captain, and another man arriving, but after that ... it's all black. How long have I been here?

Jorai frowns, but his expression clears after a moment. "Our healers spent all morning working on you. You're OK,

Kaylin. Your body—your body is healed." His voice breaks, and he squeezes my hand.

I can do nothing but stare at him as the thought slowly permeates through my tired mind. Healed. In its wake, I find a million questions rising to the surface, but I don't know which ones to ask and whether I should ask them because I still don't know what's *happening*.

Jorai knows who I am. And I remember him calling me a slave. But he's holding my hand. And looking at me like he did while we danced. Like when we were children. Like I dreamed.

I slowly pull my hand from his, even though it's like stabbing my own heart, and force myself to sit up against the headboard. My hair feels like a mess, and I resist the urge to run a hand through it. This has to be said.

Jorai sits on the edge of the bed, watching me cautiously, his expression soft but his eyes studying my every move like he's still expecting some sign of pain despite his words.

"Jory—Jorai," I correct, "I'm not a princess. I'm not even fae."

"I don't care." He shakes his head. "I never cared. Not when you were a maid's daughter, not when you were a fae princess, and not when you were a slave."

"I still am," I say, fiddling with my shirt and trying to ignore the watery blur forming in my eyes.

"You *were*," he says firmly, but his fingers are gentle as he tilts my face up to look at him. "I have always loved you, Kaylin. I never stopped thinking of you, even when I thought I'd never see you again. If you can forgive me, I never want to be parted from you again."

A tear spills over and runs down my cheek but I frown, searching his earnest eyes. "Forgive you?"

"For not coming for you at Zianne's. For not *seeing* you at the festival. And for being the biggest fool in all of Ashennor for thinking everything was alright in this kingdom."

My lips part, and for a full minute I can do nothing but stare at him. At Prince Jorai, the boy *I* have never stopped thinking about. The boy that *I* love. But I can't let myself bask in this moment as much as I desperately want to.

I shake my head slowly. "I still have a debt to pay."

"What?" His brows crease in confusion.

"Zianne," I say, "I'm paying off my father's debt to her. And I'm still her daughter legally."

"She bought you as a slave, Kaylin, and I'd wager you'd be able to confirm that she was a part of the rebels too?" There's an edge to Jorai's voice, but it's not aimed at me.

I offer a slight nod.

"She has no claim to you by blood or law. Her own rights are void by her actions and you've more than paid off that debt in blood anyway." He takes my hand again. "If you don't want me—" he swallows thickly "—stay here anyway. The palace was always your home."

I shake my head, and his eyes start to close off.

"No!" I say quickly, grabbing onto Jorai's hand before he can take it away. "I mean, I do. I do love you, Jory. I've loved you ever since we held hands and spun around the ballroom."

He grins, and I know he's reliving that moment from so long ago.

"I'm sorry I didn't tell you who I was," I finish in a whisper, holding his hand tucked in mine, against my chest. My eyes are starting to feel heavy again, but I don't want this moment to end. I don't want to miss another second of time with him, even if my mind is still caught in disbelief.

Jorai shifts a little closer. "I didn't love you at the festival because of what I thought you were, Kaylin. I loved you because it was *you* under there. And I will keep loving you for as long as we're given and even after that."

His hand cups my face, and I close my eyes at the touch.

I remember what it was like to be loved. Not romantically, but by my mother and Cyra. For casual contact, to be in another's presence and not be afraid, not be aware of every movement and word. I hadn't realised how much I'd missed it. The gaping hole it left behind.

"Open your eyes, Kaylin," he whispers.

Jorai's breath caresses my cheek and I open my eyes to find him only inches away.

"Will you marry me?"

I stare at him. His words bouncing around my head once, then twice.

He doesn't take them back. And I don't want him to.

"Y—yes." Because we've already loved for a lifetime. We've seen each other grow up and learn and live, and though we weren't there for all of it, he knows me. And I know him. I'd know him even if I were blind and deaf, and the whole world tried to keep us apart.

Jorai pulls back, slipping a necklace out from under his shirt, revealing a silver band with a gem of starlight in its centre and sapphires wrapping all the way around the band.

"No, Jory, not your mother's—"

He smiles, his face soft as he takes it from the chain. "I remember showing it to you that day we were hiding from your mother in the closet in my bedroom. I knew then that I wanted you to have it one day."

"You should have just asked. I probably would have said yes." I laugh, trying to hold back another tear. I wish I wasn't so tired, that half of my mind wasn't focusing on trying to stay awake.

"Better late than never," he murmurs, slipping the ring onto my finger.

Jorai's hand goes back to my face, and my heart stutters in that small, infinite moment before he presses his lips to mine.

My eyes fall closed again, and I don't ever want this moment to end as the fear and the shadow of pain finally fall away. My fingers slide into his hair as we break apart, and I smile against his lips.

"There's one more thing we need to do," he whispers.

"What?"

He pulls back. "May I?" he says gesturing to the blankets still covering my legs.

I frown but nod.

He stands, tugging the blankets back, baring my legs. My ankles. And my manacle still clamped tightly around my left one.

I feel my face redden, and I can't seem to look at Jorai.

"Kaylin," he says, gently turning my face towards him again. "I don't care." He straightens. "Besides, we're finally taking this thing off. We didn't have a key last night, but I had one made to force it open."

Jorai pulls a small silver key out from a pocket. There's nothing special about it, nothing to signify that it's about to change my life.

Grinning, Jorai slides the key into the lock and the manacle falls open on the bed. He gently moves aside the cloths left behind. A soft breeze caresses the scarred skin.

A stunned laugh slips through my lips and Jorai's smile widens, even though a shadow lingers in his eyes as they land on my scars. I stare at him with wide, disbelieving eyes, totally and completely lost for words.

"There," he says, handing me the key. I clutch it to my chest like it's one of the most precious things in the world. Second only to the ring on my hand.

"Thank you," I finally whisper, my lids growing heavy again.

Jorai's lips find mine once more.

"You have my shoe," I say, fingering the dirty slipper tucked into his belt.

"I might keep it," he laughs. "It's been there since I found it. We've been through a lot, me and this shoe." His face turns serious again and he leans forwards. "I can't believe it was you," he says against my lips. "I hoped ..."

I kiss the thought away. I hoped, too.

But the moment is ruined when I finally break into a yawn. Laughing, Jorai pulls back, his thumb caressing my cheek.

"Sleep, Kaylin. We can talk more later." He presses a gentle kiss to my forehead.

Another yawn stops my argument in its tracks.

Jorai tucks me into bed, gives my hand a squeeze, then excuses himself with one last long look my way before the curtain falls across the empty doorway behind him.

31

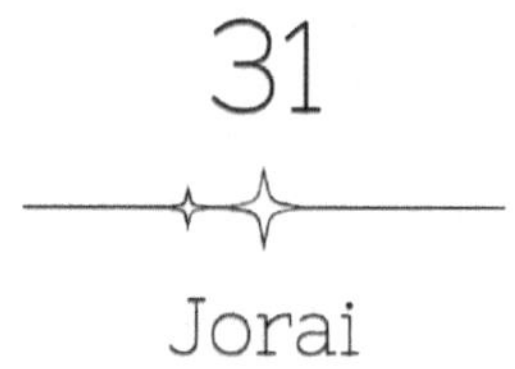

Jorai

I FIND RAIDEN IN his bedroom, his belongings spread out on the bed in front of him as he repacks his bag. Something in my chest sinks, but I knew this moment was coming. And that it would come even sooner once we found Kaylin.

"When do you leave?" I ask, pausing on the threshold.

"First light tomorrow," he says, turning to face me, his lips curving into a soft smile. "I think it's time I continue my own search."

For Princess Zara.

"Where will you start?" I ask.

"At the beginning. When the trail's gone cold, it's the best place to start."

Nodding, I cross the room, stopping in front of him.

"Thank you, Raiden," I say, though I can never thank him enough for all he's done. "If you ever need anything, anything at all, you need only ask."

"It was my pleasure. I'm glad to see the girl safe." His eyes turn thoughtful. "I'll remember your offer, though, Jorai."

"I'll look forward to it, brother." I would help this man do anything.

We grip arms, and I turn to leave the ambassador to finish preparing for his long journey home. "We'll see you at the wedding?"

Laughing, Raiden runs a hand through his short hair. "You move fast, Your Highness. I'll be there. I wouldn't want to miss another Ashennor party."

Cyra is sitting with Kaylin when I return, her eyes fixed on her sleeping goddaughter.

"She's exhausted," she whispers. I sit on the edge of the bed, looking down at my princess. The key is still clutched safely in her hand.

"She'll be OK," I say, tucking a strand of hair behind Kaylin's ear. She looks so peaceful in sleep, with all her fear and worries eased. She'll bear the signs of her slavery for life, in the old scars on her ankles and arm, but she's finally free of the nightmare.

But the sight of her in that underground room has yet to leave me, and I doubt it ever will. The smell of her blood, and the way her skin hung in ribbons—a shudder runs through me.

"Interesting jewellery she's wearing," Cyra says slyly.

"How long did it take you to notice?" I grin, my dark thoughts vanishing as my eyes land on my mother's ring.

"Oh, I smelt it on her before I even walked through the door," she laughs. If anyone could do such an impossible feat, it would be Cyra.

Her small hand takes mine, pulling my gaze away from Kaylin.

Her green eyes are shinning with a watery film. "Thank you. Thank you for saving her."

I lean over, tugging her forwards and enveloping her in a hug. There's nothing to be said in this moment, but I can feel the tension leaving my aunt's body. The fear and worry she's held onto since Kaylin was taken. Just how much of it was worsened by memories of her own ordeal years ago?

After a long moment, Cyra pulls back, and I decide to break the news to her. "Raiden's leaving."

She nods, her hair bouncing. "I know."

"You're not upset?" I ask slowly. Though I didn't think there was anything between them, the two had certainly grown close in such a short time. And while no one could replace Gaara, I'd wager that Raiden comes close to meeting him.

But Cyra playfully slaps my arm, clearly following my line of thought. "The ambassador is a good friend, and I shall miss him *as a good friend*. Besides—" she waves a hand "—he's much too young."

"Cyra ..."

She smiles a little sadly. "I had my time, and I wouldn't change it. I don't want someone to replace Gaara."

"I'm sorry," I say, watching her wipe away a single tear. "I didn't mean—"

"I know," she says, shedding the sadness that fell over her with some effort, "But I am ready for another wedding around here! It's been much too long, and you two make the perfect couple."

I grin, looking back down at Kaylin to find her sleepy eyes on me.

"I didn't get to thank him," she says, looking between me and Cyra.

I frown. "Raiden?"

She nods. "For helping me, and you."

Cyra jumps to her feet. "Well then, I'll go find him. He hasn't left just yet, darling."

"Cyra!" She sits up, grabbing my aunt's hand. "Thank you—for everything."

Cyra throws her arms around Kaylin, squeezing her tightly. "I want to know everything I've missed, darling. Everything."

Kaylin nods into her shoulder.

"I'll go find the ambassador." Cyra twists on her heel, wiping away another tear and hurrying from the room. I watch her go, sure my aunt had realised Kaylin was awake as we talked about Gaara.

I smile. Between the two of us and Zephi, we'll make this place Kaylin's home.

"What are you thinking about?" Kaylin asks, tilting her head.

"You. And how much everyone is going to love their new princess."

She smiles and I feel my chest soar and ache all at once.

"I never want to be parted from you again," I whisper.

"Then you won't," Kaylin says, leaning forwards, her eyes slipping to my lips.

And we seal her words with a kiss, a promise that goes deep into my soul and makes its home there. I fought for this girl, and I'd do it again and again until I breathe my last, just to see her smile.

Kaylin

In the morning, Jorai and I get ready to head out to farewell Raiden. But we're delayed in my room when I trip over my own feet. I'd spent nearly half my life with a weight around one ankle, and it takes my body a moment to adjust. But it's with laughter that Jory and I emerge outside. Because every trip and stumble on the way over from my room was one more reminder that it's finally gone.

The captain and Cyra are already waiting. Ambassador Raiden's horse is already saddled, his weapons strapped to the bags. Jory's mood shifts instantly.

"I'm sorry to see you go," he says, stepping forwards to clasp arms with Raiden in farewell.

"I'll be back soon," the man promises, looking between us with a smile.

I feel myself blush at the knowledge in his eyes.

"Thank you, Ambassador." I thanked him yesterday too, but I don't think I'll ever stop thanking him, or any of them. It's only been a day and I still can't believe how much has changed. "I hope you find the princess."

He grins wider. "I've found one, so I'm sure I'll find another."

I feel my blush deepen.

Cyra leaps forwards, throwing her arms around him. "Send my love to Laurel and Turin," she says, voice muffled against his broad chest.

"I will." He takes her hand as she pulls away, pressing a kiss to it. "Save me a dance at the wedding."

I look between them. After his conversation in my room with Cyra about Raiden, Jorai had explained that the ambassador was only a new acquaintance. But it's clear that the friendships these three have developed are deep.

My godmother laughs. "You can bet on that."

Raiden shakes hands with Zephi next, and then the ambassador is slipping into the saddle, and in no time at all, he's gone. Even though I didn't know the man, I feel the loss of his presence, and I know the others do, too.

Jorai and I stay outside as Cyra and Zephi head back into the palace. My gaze eventually drifts away from the road and up to the building of starlight behind me. Home.

"Kaylin," Jorai says hesitantly. "My father wants me to ask, do you know anything about the rebels? Any members we've missed or any information that could help?"

I start to shake my head but pause at a flash of memory. "Oriane likes to record gossip in a journal," I say, unsure if it might help. "She had it out in a meeting they had at the house. There could be something in there?"

Jorai smiles. "We'll check it out."

"What will happen to them?" I ask quietly.

Jory's hand slips into mine. "Prison," he says, knowing exactly who I mean. "Zianne will never leave, her use of the blood bond will see to that, but I doubt Oriane will see the light of day again. Especially if there's anything condemning in that journal."

I feel myself nod slowly. Knowing Oriane the way I do now, there is.

"Love?" Jorai prompts.

I shake myself from my thoughts, turning to him with a smile. "I guess I'm free, then."

His blue eyes soften. "Yes," he says. "And we have plenty of lost time to catch up on."

"And a wedding to plan." A nervous giggle escapes me. I'm getting married.

"And a wedding to plan."

Rising on my toes, I press my lips to his, finally daring to believe that this isn't going to end. That this is my life now. And I'm safe. I'm happy. I'm his, and he's mine.

Thank you for reading Of Glass and Cinders and coming on this journey with me.

Want to know what happened to Cyra and Gaara? Check out my free Swan Princess retelling!

Blurb:

Before she was the Fairy Godmother, she was the Swan Princess.

Bubbly Princess Cyra is being sent to a neighbouring country to prepare the way for her brother, the king. She's not to talk about the differences between their countries, and especially not about their disagreement on human slavery. But Cyra has a bone to pick with the grumpy Prince Gaara, who called her out on her 'ignorant' behaviour on her last visit. How dare he be so right. She has three goals for this trip.

1. Make Gaara smile.
2. Hold one entire conversation with him.
3. Make him see that she's changed.
And, OK,
4. See if that spark is still there.

But Cyra never makes it there. Kidnapped and trapped in her shifted form, Cyra is left behind as a swan while her attacker takes her place. A deadly plot begins to unfold. And no one suspects a thing.
Except Gaara.

Of Swans and Princes is available through my newsletter. Get it here: www.linktr.ee/tianidavids

Pronunciation guide

Names:

Jorai: Joor (like door)- I

Cyra: Sigh-ruh

Zephi: Zeph-ee

Oriane: Or-ee-arn

Zianne: Z-I-anne

Raiden: Ray-den

Eran: Erin

Laika: Lie-kuh

Locations:

Ashennor: Ashen-noor

Frigarth: Free-garth

Ellcombe: El-comb

Acknowledgements

I can't believe we're here at the end of my fourth book! (Plus my sweet, depressing little Swan Princess novella Of Swans and Princes).

Writing has been such an amazing journey, but I really couldn't do it without you. Your comments, dms, likes, and shares have meant the world to me. Thank you, thank you, thank you.

Thank you again to Jesus, for being such a wonderful comforter and friend, for planting this desire in me and for helping it come to life. Let me never lose sight of you.

The team at MoorBooks! You are amazing! Thank you for this stunning cover- I could just stare at it all day.

Ashley at Enchanted Author Co, thank you for the time you put into these edits.

My wonderful beta readers, the old and the new, thank you for your outstanding feedback and advice. I'm forever amazed at what a fresh pair of eyes can see!

Tiani Davids grew up in Victoria reading middle-grade and young adult fantasy, a love that soon expanded to include writing. She now lives on the Far South Coast of New South

Wales where she cultivates her passion for reading, writing, and all things Tolkien.

Connect with Tiani:

Instagram: @tianidavids

Facebook: @authortianidavids